Professor Schmoot Has Lost His Keys Again

Professor Schmoot Has Lost His Keys Again

CHRISTOPHER MORSE

RESOURCE *Publications* • Eugene, Oregon

PROFESSOR SCHMOOT HAS LOST HIS KEYS AGAIN

Resource Publications
An Imprint of Wipf and Stock Publishers
199 W. 8th Ave., Suite 3
Eugene, OR 97401

www.wipfandstock.com

PAPERBACK ISBN:978-1-5326-1746-1
HARDCOVER ISBN: 978-1-4982-4215-8
EBOOK ISBN: 978-1-4982-4214-1

Manufactured in the U.S.A.   SEPTEMBER 15, 2017

Cover artwork inspired by a sketch by Roland Bainton of the author as a beginning seminary student in 1960

To the members of the Inkpots Writing Group,
who listened to the first episode
and urged me to pursue where it might lead:
Craig Berggren, Carol Conway, David Hirschman,
and Tom Miller.

Contents

Cast of Characters
(In Order of Appearance)

Mildred Castleton—Granddaughter of the original founder of the seminary that became Star-Cross and, as the inheritor of the Castleton legacy, the school's essential benefactor.

Tucker Upton Schmoot—Trusted professor called upon by the president to carry out his administrative ideas and the one around whom most of the action centers.

Byah Longshot—Former ashram director in India and currently the president of Star-Cross Spirituality Seminary, a school with postmodern aspirations confounded by financial and academic deficits.

Clarence—Longtime Castleton family chauffeur of Mildred Castleton.

Isadora Broadside—Outspoken professor of Asian contemplation and peace activist.

Wisteria Dean—The interim administrative CEO appointed to serve while the president was away on sabbatical.

Wetmore Readily—The name of the seminary physician whose signature was required for approval on all student *LIQ* medical requests for exemptions from grading because of *Low Interest Quotient.*

The Titteley Sisters, Trudila and Frutila—Identical twin instructors of spiritual retreat workshops hired by Star-Cross as visiting adjuncts for a one year *joint*, mistakenly publicized as conjoined, appointment.

Angelica Blankchek—A student.

Brother John—Director of the *Center for Religious Assessment Policies* and outside consultant.

Batson Belfry—Youngest and most recently hired faculty member in New Testament.

Rigore Mortisse—Inflexible seminary librarian.

Ferdinand Lyzer—Popularly known as *Ferdie,* campus groundskeeper and tender of the Sacred Garden.

Daphne Doolittle—Chair of the Star-Cross Board of Directors and online marketer of high energy products having little apparent effect upon her tenure as presiding officer.

Episode 1

Mildred Castleton's Periodic Visit

THE DAY HAD ARRIVED for one of Mildred Castleton's periodic visits to the seminary, and Professor Tucker U. Schmoot, or T. Upton Schmoot as he preferred to be addressed, anticipated it with his usual apprehension. The fact was that he did not like being deceptive. The school was dependent upon the Castleton Family Trust for its survival, and this meant keeping the venerable lady oblivious to how much the place had changed from the theological seminary she loved to recall that her grandfather had first endowed for the training of evangelists and missionaries over a century ago. Of the current faculty only Tucker had been around long enough to remember when that original seminary, whose grounds they currently occupied, was still in existence. President Longshot, who was a relative newcomer eager to shape the place in a very different image, had urged upon him the distasteful, but admittedly essential, responsibility for hosting the devoted benefactor's lucrative visits and nurturing her pious, if false, impressions. If all this seemed more than faintly unethical—"Get ready to set up your Potemkin village again," President Longshot with a wink would mutter to him—Tucker would remind himself not to be too moralistic. The need was great, and the resources were there.

Less than twenty years old, the present seminary desperately needed to keep the old Castleton money pump running. It had morphed out of what had once been two conservative Bible colleges it now preferred to forget that had been located not far from each other. One had been independent and fundamentalist and gone by the name Star of Bethlehem. The other, which was the one Mildred's grandfather had founded, was socially more upscale and doctrinaire. It had prided itself on what it called its Old School Reformed traditions and initially had been chartered as the Cross of Calvary Reformed School, a name later abbreviated to dispel public misunderstanding simply to Calvary Cross. In the cultural climate of the late sixties they had each lost their students, their accreditation, and, indeed for most all concerned, their point. Star of Bethlehem had no buildings of value, but it occupied salable land that its trustees put on the market. Calvary Cross's campus stood vacant, but the Castletons saw to the upkeep of its Gothic structures, and kept the grounds mowed in hopes for a better day. That day came with the consolidation of both schools' holdings and their subsequent rechartering on the Calvary campus as Star-Cross Theological Seminary. The newly formed board of trustees had argued at length over the choice of a name and had finally settled for the least parochial sense from each of the two school's former names, agreeing only on the hyphenated Star-Cross.

President Longshot, whose previous career had been in conducting ashrams in India under his Hindi first name *Byah*, had subsequently advocated for the less dogmatic sounding term "Spirituality" in the seminary's title, and thus the word "Theological" was dropped as well. Even so, the name *Star-Cross Spirituality Seminary* had still continued to offend some of the more gender aware members of the faculty who pointed out the discriminatory etymological derivation of the word "seminary" from "seminal," and hence "semen," with the sexist effect, even if unconscious, this derivation would have upon attracting a desirable constituency. But on this matter the President had urged caution for the time being, mindful that Mildred Castleton might not understand.

As punctual as clockwork the old Castleton Chrysler wound its way up the hill to the seminary's main entrance where Tucker stood ready once again to extend the seminary's welcome. Mildred's faithful driver Clarence had been with the family for most of his life, his father having been employed by the Castletons before him. Tucker had never known them to be late, and though both had slowed some with age in their advancing years, they still made an impressive appearance as the ever devoted Clarence steadied his matron out of the car and onto Tucker's arm to be escorted into the President's office. The routine which never varied would consist of tea served elegantly by the seminary kitchen staff all in rented formal waiter attire, followed by the President's ever glowing report of the seminary's progress, concluding with a not so subtle pitch for some major financial donation.

"What we most need," President Longshot confided in his most ingratiating manner, "is a renovation of our chapel. Indeed that would mean so much to our students."

At first the dear lady preoccupied with sipping her tea appeared not to hear him so Longshot repeated the comment in a slightly louder voice. "Oh yes," Mildred suddenly took notice, setting her tea cup down, "the Major's Chapel! I haven't been there in years. Could someone take me to see it? I want to see the Major's Chapel."

Tucker looked at the President with dismay. How could the man be so uninformed as not to know that the old chapel where long forgotten revivals were once held a century ago had originally been named for Mildred's father, Major Castleton. The plaque over the door designating the Major Castleton Chapel had been one of the first remnants from the old evangelical Calvary Cross Seminary removed when the new Star-Cross was founded. Tucker had long since lost his own keys to it and doubted that President Longshot, and indeed most of the current faculty, had even been aware of the chapel's history. Furthermore, Star-Cross had effectively done away with worship services in any form that Mildred might recognize from its old Reformed days, and Tucker was not at all sure if the largely disregarded location once named for the

Major was even open for them to see. But Mrs. Castleton had suddenly become alive with eager anticipation and struggled to raise herself from her chair and reach for Tucker's arm to be conducted to revisit the old chapel.

Longshot, sensing the near crisis his comment had precipitated, urged everyone to please be seated for a moment so that he could explain how the chapel now functioned and why new funds were so necessary for its restoration. A fresh cup of tea was thrust upon Mildred as she was passed another tray of biscuits.

The truth of the matter was this, but of course it could not be divulged to the Castleton Trust. The once Gothic chapel originally named for the Major with its stained glass windows of Martin Luther and John Calvin had long since been designated to become known more inclusively as the Star-Cross Self-Expression Center. There were no longer regular worship services of the kind involving scriptural readings, sermons, or prayers, and the only policy guideline regarding meditation that the faculty had been able to agree on was that self-expressions of interiority and self-expressions of exteriority both be encouraged. More recently, however, a controversy had arisen over a proposal to supplement the dead white male stained glass windows of Eurocentric Protestantism, as critics referred to them, by commissioning an equal sized portrayal of Pope Joan's image to counterbalance the ones of Luther and Calvin.

Known in history as the only female pope, but disputed by historians as being merely a legend, Pope Joan is pictured in folklore as heading the papacy in Rome between the years 855–857. She is best remembered as disguising herself as a man and working her way up the Vatican hierarchy until after finally becoming cardinal and then pope she inadvertently gave birth to a child while mounting a horse and was dragged to her death. (Cf. John Julius Norwich, *Absolute Monarchs: A History of the Papacy*, Random House: 2011, pp. 63–70.) Those advocating for a new stained glass window with her image argued that it would make the Self-Expression Center more fully inclusive in gender and spirituality by introducing a female from a non-Protestant tradition whose secret pregnancy provides an icon for all historically invalidated and similarly rejected women in subverting the authority of a male dominated ecclesiasticism.

When several of the more staid members of the history department objected that none of the fictions of Pope Joan could be documented as fact, the postmodernist cultural theorists heatedly reminded them that fact/fiction binaries no longer apply in matters of spiritual self-expression.

Tucker Schmoot had remained silent in this controversy and now he wondered how President Longshot would attempt to extract from the Castleton Trust funds for this new stained glass window without divulging to the Major's daughter the real aim of his fraudulent deception. Luckily, Mildred suddenly seemed to forget her request for a visit to the chapel and shortly called for Clarence to bring up the Chrysler and drive her home. Tucker dutifully helped her to the car, and walking back across campus reaffirmed his resolve once again never to do the President's bidding in this shameful manner.

Episode 2

Cornerstone Laying for the New Chapel

WITH THE PASSAGE OF months since Mildred Castleton's last visit to the seminary, and further negotiations with the lawyers of the Castleton Trust, a sufficient sum of money had been granted for the reconstruction of a virtually new chapel. In fact, it was more than sufficient. President Longshot's deceptiveness had been so successful in appealing to Mildred's devotion to her father, for whom the old chapel, once called "The Major's Chapel," had been named, that the forthcoming grant had exceeded the initial request. "I want it done right for Papa," Mildred had stipulated. "The Major's Chapel, like the Major himself, must stand as the best."

The expenditure had aroused considerable competition among the various departments of the faculty since all realized that in the present seminary whatever was designated as the chapel facility, whether "The Old Major's" or not, would actually be space used for other purposes. As the day approached for the official laying of a new cornerstone the planning committee had even reached an impasse over whether the announced theme of the public occasion should be "The Spirituality of Matter" or "The Materiality of Spirit." Vigorous arguments by the more aesthetically minded were countered by those of the more socio-ethically minded, and once again President Longshot had summoned Tucker to come to the rescue. His assignment was to arrange a ceremony that would navigate these currents of division on the faculty and at the same time do nothing that would upset the hallowed memories of their benefactor upon whom they all were dependent. The window to Pope Joan would not be installed until later.

Tucker first managed to get the faculty, however grudgingly, to acknowledge that for the sake of the Castleton Fund the theme for the occasion of the chapel's new cornerstone laying would at least have to sound biblical, and after more deliberation his proposal of "The Wind Bloweth Where It Will" had been agreed to. Yet a further predicament arose when Mildred suddenly requested that her father's favorite hymn be sung, "In The Cross of Christ I Glory." This time there was adamant opposition to the mention of "Christ" since the seminary was officially attempting in all its publications to shed itself of any spiritual exclusivity. The President and most members of the faculty had never heard of the hymn, and Tucker was called upon to relate its exact words and alter them sufficiently so that they could be sung by a soloist with muffled diction but not printed as a hymn in the official program for all in attendance to see. Thus he arranged for, "In the Cross of Christ I glory, towering o'er the wrecks of time" to become, with the soloist's subtly muffled diction, a reference to the seminary, "In Star-Cross's new life I glory, towering o'er the wrecks of time," while the second line, "All the light of sacred story gathers round *His* head sublime," was easily adjusted to, "All the light of sacred story gathers round *this* head sublime."

To Tucker's great relief on the day of the ceremony itself, as he and the President were escorting Mildred to an honored seat on the rostrum, she confided in a stage whisper to him that she had forgotten to bring her hearing aid and would need him to repeat for her what was being said. So it was that, following the President's opening remarks, "We meet today in recognition that it is neither the spirituality of materiality, nor the materiality of spirituality alone, but both together, that is the cornerstone of our life today in a postmodern world," the dear lady smiled contentedly as the ever resourceful

Professor T. Upton Schmoot translated into her eagerly waiting ear, "We meet today in recognition that Jesus Christ himself is the chief cornerstone, and that no other stone can be laid except that which has been laid, none other than the name of Jesus."

Episode 3

Flight to Support Native American Land Rights

THE PRESIDENT'S CALL HAD not come to him until after 11 pm, just as Tucker was about to turn off his bedside reading lamp for the night. It had been a long day with all the cornerstone laying ceremonies for the new chapel and, now with a break before summer school classes were to begin, he had looked forward to sleeping late in the morning. But the President, who always spoke as if somewhat excited, had sounded on the phone even more so, and Tucker sat up in bed to make sure he was wide awake and was hearing him correctly.

"I need you for a special mission," Longshot was saying, without pausing to acknowledge the lateness of the hour. "Tomorrow we have the chance to get the seminary's name associated with some of the country's most prestigious environmental groups, and I want you to represent us. You are the only one who can really impress them, Tucker, you really are, so I want you to do this for Star-Cross."

Not waiting for a word of response, Longshot hurriedly continued. If Tucker had not known that the president religiously abstained from all alcohol, he would have been sure that Longshot was well into his cups. "It'll not only mean publicity for the school, Tucker, we are talking about the possibility of increased enrollment and funding for Star-Cross's endowment. This could really be the start of a whole new future for us. Are you getting the point of what I am talking about, Tucker? This is really big. Just imagine, I can see it now. We have never had such an opportunity for this kind of national recognition. And that's what we need to join the big leagues, Tucker, national recognition. We've got the chance to build a national reputation as a leading center of support for Native American sacred land spirituality and eco-friendly environmentalism. This is the coming trend, Tucker, there is big money here."

Getting up before dawn in a state of high anxiety after a sleepless night, Tucker tried to make sense of the details of what the President was asking him to do as he rushed to prepare for this new assignment. Apparently, Longshot had learned over the Internet of a major rally of eco-friendly spirituality and environmental groups to protest new contracts for oil drilling in lands considered sacred to local Indian tribes. Requests had gone out for supporters, and Longshot had managed to get a speaker from Star-Cross onto the program. Tucker had been astounded to learn that the event in question was a half continent away in Williston, North Dakota, and that he would have to be there in time for the ceremony declaring the oil lands a sacred territory that was to take place with tribal dancing promptly at sundown. Longshot had told him he had quickly arranged through Mildred Castleton for a private plane from the Castleton Trust to fly him to Williston, a trip that the pilot estimated would take about five hours one way, given the plane currently available. Longshot had assured Tucker that he would have plenty of time while on route to prepare his remarks about how Star-Cross stands for earth spirituality and that an early ride had been ordered for him to a nearby airfield where the Castleton plane would be waiting for him.

The plane turned out to be an antique model propjet that reminded Tucker of Mildred Castleton's older Chrysler, and there was enough turbulence on route to maintain his feeling of trepidation. The solitary pilot sat directly in front of him but the noise made any conversation between them impossible.

Tucker tried to concentrate on the information he had quickly been able to search on his laptop before leaving. It seemed that oil shale had first been discovered around Williston in 1951 and within forty-five days over 30 million acres of North Dakota had been leased for drilling out of the total 44.8 million acres that made up the whole state. By the end of 2010 over 458,000 barrels of oil had been produced with 2 to 3 billion barrels estimated by the United States Geodetic Service to be still in the ground and recoverable with the application of the latest technology. Native American resentment at this intrusion in these lands traditionally considered sacred had been the motivation for this national protest rally.

As the plane circled the landing strip in Williston, Tucker could see a large number gathered on the ground below and in the near distance the oil rigs in operation. They touched down within full view of the crowd and taxied over to a stop directly in front of a huge billboard. Tucker with relief thanked the pilot for finding their way.

"Oh, no problem, Professor," he said. "I fly up here a lot. The Castleton Trust has a major investment in these oil companies. You probably noticed we have our own parking space right here in front of our big advertizing sign for *Castleton Fracking*."

Episode 4

Mix-up on Plaque to Honor Mildred Castleton

MORE THAN A YEAR had passed since the seminary had hosted a visit for Mildred Castleton, and unfortunately for the school its dependence upon its chief and, for all practical purposes, sole benefactor had not lessened. T. Upton kept in touch with the dear lady thorough occasional notes and phone calls so it was not unexpected that President Longshot continued to rely on him whenever the need for revenue became most urgent.

Tucker chafed at the compliant role expected of him in these beguiling attempts to drain more money from the Castleton Trust, but he told himself that Star-Cross would be no worse a depository for Mildred's fortune than some hitherto unknown distant nieces and nephews, or long lost neglectful cousins, who most predictably would show up at mourning time to claim their inheritance when she passed away.

Longshot's latest ploy, as if the disastrous misadventure to North Dakota had not been enough, had so barely missed becoming a catastrophe that even now, some weeks later, Tucker still shuttered to think of what had been averted. It had been President Longshot's idea to arrange a banquet in Mildred's honor at which she would be presented with an impressive plaque praising her contributions to the life of Star-Cross. The real intent was evident in the assignment he gave to Tucker to suggest a flattering scriptural verse to be engraved on the plaque, something hagiographic enough, as Longshot expressed it, to loosen up the Castleton money bags once again.

Tucker was instructed to phone in his chosen verse to the President's office where Longshot's secretary, who was as uninformed of such scriptural matters as her boss, would then proceed from there with the necessary banquet preparations. After pondering his displeasing task, Tucker decided on words from the *Gospel of John* as most appropriate and honestly reflective of Mildred's generosity, and he phoned Longshot's office secretary with the message that the text to be used was *John* 14, verse 17.

> This is the Spirit of truth, whom the world cannot receive, because it neither sees him nor knows him. You know him because he abides with you, and will be in you.

He had grimaced at the thought of how Longshot would probably not sense the irony of how this verse was in contrast to him. But then, Tucker reminded himself, who was he to feel superior?

The day arrived with several hundred guests present to pay tribute to Mildred. They cared less for Star-Cross, which most of them only knew by sight driving by, than for the Castleton name and reputation with which they were eager by association to enhance their own social position.

Before the presentation, just as the guests were about to be directed to their places at the handsomely set banquet tables, Tucker to his great alarm discovered the error. On each place card was engraved a facsimile of the plaque to be presented and under Mildred's name this verse was printed in her honor: not *John* 14:7, but *John* 4:7.

> The woman said to Jesus, "I have no husband." Jesus said to her, "You are right in saying 'I have no husband,' for you have had five husbands, and the one you have now is not your husband.'"

Seized with sudden panic, before the guests could find their places and before Mildred had been seated, Tucker swept up and down the flower strewn tables retrieving each place card before anyone had seen it. He had managed to do this in such a graceful, unobtrusive manner that, with a maestro's wave of his arm, he made it look as if everyone was conducted to sit wherever they wished. When he was able to reach Longshot's ear he whispered to him to announce that the plaque was still at the engravers and would be presented at a later time because our dear Mrs. Castleton was a more fitting living embodiment of benevolence and generosity than any engraved plaque could ever be. The guests applauded these words warmly while Mildred protested with modest delight, "O my, my! You know I'm only too happy to further the Lord's work whenever I can."

Episode 5

Isadora Broadside's Peace Seekers and the Militarized Buddha

Isadora Broadside, for all her talk of peace and compassion, was not one to let a grievance pass, and Tucker dreaded the suddenly called meeting of the Star-Cross faculty that she had demanded that the President convene for later in the afternoon. Professor Broadside, he could understand, was rightly upset. The meditation seminar on peace through nonviolence that she had been planning for months had been scheduled for the day before, with bus loads of "peace seekers," as they called themselves, arriving from the surrounding area, with some even as far as a hundred miles away. Indeed the seminary had promoted the occasion all semester with extensive publicity. It was to be the signal event held on campus in the newly remodeled Self-Expression Center, now designed with little resemblance to the chapel used for the training of evangelists and missionaries in the old Reformed seminary of Calvary Cross from which the present Star-Cross had its origins. What had so inflamed Professor Broadside was a confluence of circumstances that only Tucker, President Longshot, and the campus grounds-keeper were aware of, but could not reveal. An unanticipated call from Mildred Castleton the previous morning had indicated that she had heard reports of the landscaping around the chapel and was planning to have her driver Clarence bring her by to take a look. For some time the steps had made it difficult for her to get out of the car for tea in the president's office, as had been the custom, and by her own admission her eyesight was failing. On the false assumption that his aging benefactor would no longer be making excursions to the campus, Longshot had prominently installed a Buddha statue as part of the new landscaping in proximity to the Self-Expression Center. His urgent message to Tucker was that he come without delay to the Center to assist the grounds-superintendent whom Longshot had just dispatched from his office with, in his words to Tucker, "some camouflage to disguise the Compassionate One beyond recognition before Castleton arrives."

Not knowing what to expect, Tucker had hurried to the Center, where he found the grounds-keeper securing a Halloween type infantry helmet on the nonresistant Buddha and strapping a play musket across its placid front. No sooner had they militarized the Buddha than the Castleton Chrysler as if on cue made its way up the hill and stopped, some distance from the chapel entrance. Tucker motioned to Clarence not to drive closer and came and got into the back seat with Mildred, pointing out to her the shadowy outline of the statue among the new shrubbery in the distance.

"Oh, Professor Schmoot," she cried, squinting through her dark glasses. "You hadn't told me it's the Major! I can tell it's Papa. I can see his helmet. Oh, how wonderful that the seminary is honoring dear Papa's service in this way."

Incredibly, just as her satisfied visit ended and the Chrysler departed, the caravan of "peace seekers" had arrived at the chapel entrance and to the near apoplexy of the welcoming committee led by Professor Broadside and her associates they embarked from the busses only to face a Buddha in military gear.

Tucker and the grounds-man had managed to hide away from all the commotion without being noticed. But the distraught professor, convinced that a student prank had been perpetrated to humiliate her, demanded that the President and faculty find out who had instigated this sacrilege and expel those responsible immediately from the seminary. Tucker wondered what a called faculty meeting could achieve, but feigning innocence he had resolved to demonstrate sympathetic support of Broadside by seconding any motion designed to placate her, whatever it was.

Tucker had been impressed with how well the President had maneuvered the faculty at the special meeting demanded by Broadside's near hysterical insistence that the culprit, whoever it was, be expelled from Star-Cross at once. Most of the seminary faculty appeared indifferent to any matters that did not invade their turf, and Isadora they considered to be a bit of a prima donna. Most of all, they resented having to come to a special faculty meeting at her calling. Longshot, in presiding, had pretended at the outset to share her shock and dismay at this unacceptable happening and expressed his personal empathy for the embarrassment it must have caused the professor with so many attendees arriving for her meditation seminar on peace through nonviolence. Tucker, sitting on the sidelines, observed with a bemused sense of amazement Longshot's incredible capacity for subterfuge. The others, as far as he could tell, cared little and simply wanted to get the meeting over. The result was that after first soothing Professor Broadside's feelings of insult, and insisting that every effort would be made to discover the culprit in this terrible sacrilege, Longshot had asked that a further measure of compensation be voted on. He proposed that the entire grounds around the Self-Expression Center be re-landscaped to add a sacred rock garden and that authentic Asian lotus plants be ordered and placed to provide a sheltering arbor for the Buddha. Several faculty members questioned whether this new allocation of seminary funds would take money from other projects in their areas that had previously been approved, but after emphatic assurances from Longshot that he would find new money the proposal had passed, following Tucker's second.

Tucker had felt a twinge of his old guilt in suspecting immediately the President's plan. Longshot would go back to the Castleton Trust yet again to solicit additional money for this so-called Sacred Garden. And again, Mildred Castleton would not be told the real reason for this further expenditure.

But now with the passage of time, the price of keeping Isadora Broadside quiet, or relatively so, had seemed worth it. And the dear benefactor, in her generosity, had not only consented to Longshot's entreaty, she had volunteered to order an impressive bronze marker to stand at the pathway of entrance into the Sacred Garden.

Some weeks had passed when Tucker found himself summoned yet again to the President's office on what was described as a confidential matter of great importance requiring his immediate assistance. The sound of agitation was clear in Longshot's voice, but all he would divulge over the phone was for Tucker to come as soon as possible.

"Schmoot," the president had greeted him, "you have got to do something!" Taking him into his inner office, away from the sight of even his staff, Longshot tore back the huge carton that had earlier been delivered containing the bronze marker that Mildred Castleton had ordered. In eye-catching bold letters its inscription read, "THIS WAY TO THE SACRED GARDEN OF GETHSEMANE."

Episode 6

Wisteria Dean's Interim Management of Star-Cross

It was while President Longshot was in India on a half year leave from the seminary that Tucker Schmoot suddenly found himself caught up in circumstances that were none of his doing. Longshot had left for India two months previously to conduct a series of his money raising ashrams for very wealthy American tourists eager to invest in four day meditation retreats on what Longshot called "the spirituality of poverty" that had been his business before coming to Star-Cross. Ostensibly his reason was the necessity of securing much needed additional revenue for the seminary, which continued to run an unsustainable deficit. Not only were alumni contributions, both in number and amount, at an all time low, dissatisfaction within the current student body over the grading system indicated that this lack of financial support would continue, at least into the immediate future. The very idea that spirituality could be made subject to academic grading was at the root of the student complaints. The effort to redress these problems—both the financial crisis and the student unrest—is what had led to Star-Cross's risk of major scandal. Through constant texted messaging and phone calls Longshot in effect had directed Tucker to arrange a cover-up.

The root of the whole matter had to do with Longshot's decision before he left for India to bring in a chief administrator unknown to the seminary community to run the place during his absence. Tucker had had serious doubts about the wisdom of this decision at the time, but Longshot in his most persuasive manner had assured the skeptical faculty members and staff that it would mean less work for each of them and that the particular individual of his choice, a Dr. Wisteria Dean, possessed a very successful record as an interim academic CEO. Tucker had therefore simply assumed, along with most everyone else, that the seminary could manage to live with this arrangement since it would only be for half a year. This assumption was soon shattered when Tucker discovered, by Longshot's own confidential admission, that the President had selected the new administrator hurriedly by browsing the Internet and had actually only met with the candidate once in person very briefly before appointing her.

The earliest hint that there might be problems occurred almost immediately when the new administrative appointee the first day after moving into her office announced that her role and title was to be that of Dean. Not only was this viewed by the faculty as the height of academic arrogance, since they had not even been consulted, the title of Dean Dean had proved so awkward to pronounce that even addressing the woman by name at all tended to be avoided as much as possible. Around the school, whispered comments circulated about "Hysteria Dean Dean" but were kept out of earshot.

Dean Dean's first idea in office to increase Star-Cross's revenue stream had been to announce on her own authority with much fanfare, including a press release and advertisement in the local papers, that a series of retreat tours of the newly landscaped grounds of the seminary would be open to the public. Special rates would be available for tour buses and organizations such as garden clubs, landscape artists, and religious groups. Designated as *Criss-Cross Tours* the project, however, had abruptly been cancelled due to a most unfortunate situation that only subsequently had come to light.

Several years earlier a local convent, long a subject of questionable reputation in the eyes of more conservative Catholics, had been disbanded upon being excommunicated by the Vatican and had contributed its reliquary of the remains of its founder, venerated as St. Fabula of Amazonia, to the seminary for safe-keeping. Critics had doubted whether Sister Fabula had ever existed except in the mystical fantasies of the nuns' order that had audaciously designated itself by the name of *The Amazon Sisters of St. Fabula*. Certainly no St. Fabula was officially recognized in the Church's calendar of saints. But since the rebellious convent upon disbanding had offered to bequeath a not insignificant endowment to Star-Cross in return for the upkeep of a display case for its revered founder's sacred relics, President Longshot had eagerly accepted their offer.

With the commencement of the campus tours, however, and the increasing public notoriety these tours created by publicizing Star-Cross as a place of sacred pilgrimage and retreat, questions soon arose about where the remains of St. Fabula were to be found and venerated in the new Self-Expression Center. Rumors began to circulate that when the long delayed window honoring Pope Joan was finally ready to be installed the reliquary of St. Fabula had been moved aside to make room and its contents had mistakenly been intermingled with the imported rocks in the newly landscaped sacred rock garden. The endowment from the old convent intended for the perpetual upkeep and display of these remains the seminary administration had apparently thought was better spent on other things. These unverified reports had aroused such suspicion in the local community, even among those most conservative Catholics who had been happy to see the Amazon Sisters excommunicated, that the idea of a money raising *Criss-Cross Tours* was hastily abandoned by Dean Dean amidst unanswered questions to her office about what had happened to all the endowment money.

In an attempt to withstand this criticism and win student support, the Dean had next single-handedly tried to change the subject by launching a new policy devised to address the grading complaint. It was with this further misadventure, coupled with that of St. Fabula's missing parts, that Star-Cross seemed headed for a major disgrace that Longshot through his constant messaging from India was imploring Tucker to prevent.

In an effort to improve student grade levels, both individual and overall, Dean Dean had sent a number of medical reports, countersigned by the long standing seminary-approved physician, to all the faculty members that forbade them from failing any in their classes, and even exempted them from grading, if they had a medically certified LIQ. The LIQ, which stood for "low interest quotient" certification, overnight became the diagnosis of over one third of the Star-Cross student body and was made retroactive, by the Dean's office, for two years previously. Since the seminary physician, Dr. Wetmore Readily, had never interfered previously in school policy by certifying such exemptions, and indeed had not even been seen around the seminary in most people's recent memory, the amount of seminary funds the Dean's office had withdrawn to pay his fees for providing such a large number of LIQ medical certifications raised disturbing questions.

Before Longshot in India had even been apprised of this second development Tucker decided on his own to consult in confidence the only source he knew he could trust. Paying an afternoon courtesy call to the delight of Mildred Castleton, Tucker inquired casually, without divulging any of the seminary's threatened scandals, if she often saw these days the seminary's old physician, Dr. Readily.

"O, dear Wetmore you mean?" Mildred smiled sadly. "Didn't you know, Professor Schmoot? He died over a year ago. My, how we all do miss him so."

With the hasty return of President Longshot, who had abruptly cut short his six month sabbatical in India after hearing from Tucker of Wisteria Dean's shocking malfeasance, Star-Cross had, to all appearances, settled back into its semester routines with the student body quite satisfied with the new inflated grading system, which put everyone in the top category of highest grade excellence—either because of ability or of grade exemption by their newly certified condition of LIQ (Low Interest Quotient). Further, the entire community remained unaware of the financial fraud that Tucker had helped the President manage to keep hidden from public notice. This was achieved, however, at Longshot's insistence that no charges be filed against Wisteria Dean on the condition that she resign immediately and make no public statement against the seminary. Dean herself had indignantly maintained, when confronted, that the whole matter had all been an innocent accounting error for which she bore no responsibility. To avoid being legally charged and its attendant publicity she had been granted the option of immediate resignation with the usual face saving explanation of moving on to greater career opportunities. As far as the suddenness of her departure was concerned, no one had raised questions now that Longshot had returned, or seemed much to care. But between the unaccountable loss of the endowment funds that had been bequeathed to the seminary by the Vatican's closing of the Convent of the Amazon Sisters of St. Fabula for the express purpose of safeguarding their namesake's relics (now seemingly having vanished amidst the dirt of the rock garden) and the missing payments bearing the deceased Dr. Readily's forged signature, the total amount of the imbalanced accounts, Tucker figured, must have been exorbitant. Yet Longshot was adamant that the matter be kept quiet for the good of the seminary's reputation, and he was emphatic with Tucker that all accounting details would be dealt with solely by the President's office.

Episode 7

Star-Cross Redefines its Curriculum: Titteley Twins' Joint Appointment

As the semester progressed and the weeks passed Tucker felt the relief of having less demands on his time coming from the President's office. He sought to steer clear of Longshot as much as possible. His own academic responsibilities required his attention, and he did not want the faculty to begin to think of him simply as Longshot's favored confidante. As one of the faculty members who had been around longest he needed to build relationships with the newer members. Their differences were not so much in age as in the ideas each held about the kind and quality of institution a seminary such as Star-Cross should be.

Tucker had grown to have a grudging affection for the place, he had to admit to himself, despite the zaniness he felt it sometimes represented. Often in the early evenings, when classes had ended and he had no meetings, he would drive alone along the narrow, back country roads that surrounded Star-Cross with no particular destination in mind. It was his favorite time to relax and regain perspective. Lying in a rolling stretch of rural woodland interspersed only by an occasional shallow lake or pond the area could boast no spectacular scenery, but there was a calming influence in the very ordinariness of the twilight landscape that he increasingly had come to rely upon as a dependable preserve.

At school so much seemed rudderless and in flux. With its decline in revenues Star-Cross had been forced to draw increasingly upon short-term, adjunct appointments in maintaining its teaching staff. The senior faculty resented the influx of these new comers and with some justification worried about their lack of scholarly credentials. The seminary had already been put on notice that it risked losing its accreditation. Some of those newly hired to teach met none of the traditionally prescribed standards. They had not only failed to complete advanced degrees in their areas, they had not even started them. In fact, the question of what the proper academic areas were for a seminary curriculum today had become a chief source of faculty disputes.

The traditional curricular divisions of the Biblical, Historical, Theological, and Practical fields that had served to classify seminary courses in the past, including those at Star of Bethlehem and Calvary Cross a half century ago, had summarily been rejected as too religiously exclusivist and outmoded following Star-Cross's founding. This was reflected in the faculty's inability even to agree upon a mission statement more specific than the italicized words of small print on the first page of the school catalogue, that "Star-Cross stands for both the spirituality of matter and the materiality of spirit in a common commitment subject to interpretation as every individual sees fit." Under such a broad umbrella of mission all applicants who had the necessary funds were assured that they would be admitted and have their personal interests accommodated without recognizing any drip line.

Tucker himself had sat through hours of faculty attempts to reconceive and rename these older curricular divisions. The current school catalogue had changed the heading of his own Biblical field as a New Testament scholar to first, Sacred Literatures, then Comparative Scriptures, to the now latest title of *Comparative Hegemonics*. This pretentious label had been insisted upon by its advocates for allegedly being more acceptable in today's postmodern culture where no discourse could claim authority or hegemony, except of course—so Tucker would chuckle to himself—the discourse of postmodernism itself. In addition, all history courses were now listed more polemically as *Deconstructive History*, theology courses had become *Spiritual Psychology* in order to be more inclusive of non-theists who increasingly were taking offense at any hint of *theos* as imperialistic god-talk. The fourth field, formerly known as the Practical Field, or Practice of Ministry, was now renamed less simply as *Experiential Modalities and Practices*.

Such was the setting in which the Titteley sisters arrived to offer their two semester workshop on what they called *Affectional Transferences* for which they had lately received popular notice on the spiritual retreat circuit where one member of the Star-Cross board of trustees had encountered their sessions and insisted that they be invited for a year at Star-Cross. The sisters were identical twins so alike in appearance that Tucker Schmoot confessed he could not tell one from the other by looking at them. They were also inseparable, with one never appearing without the other or in company with anyone else. An embarrassing oversight by the President's secretary had publicized their appointment as conjoined, rather than joint, resulting in a deluge of requests from outsiders to audit their course. In manner, they were quite different, however, with Trudila being clearly the dominant one and her sister Frutila serving more as assistant. These were ancestral names their retreat literature had explained, with the added request that the sisters be addressed more informally in their affectional workshops simply as Trudy and Fruty. In submitting their Affectional Transference course prospectus they had initially titled the first semester *From Me to You: Derivations of the Self-in-Relation*. The second semester, with no specified addition in assignments, had been titled *From You Back to Me: Reversals of Receptivity*.

When confusion was expressed in the faculty curriculum committee as to what exactly this meant and where such a course offering should properly be listed, there was sharp disagreement. No one wanted to appear ignorant of the latest trends in popular retreat culture. The Comparative Hegemonics faculty first suggested that the Tittiley offering be listed somewhat biblically as, perhaps, *The Song of Songs Revisited*. This met with resistance from the Deconstructive Historians who argued that a more proper listing reflective of their area of study would be *Repressed Affections in Suppressed Traditions*. The once theological field, now relabeled as Spiritual Psychology, insisted that such a title made the course sound more political than the Tittileys had clearly intended and suggested the compromise title of *Liberating Jung from Freud*. This left only the fourth field of Experiential Modalities and Practices, and its suggestion of *Practices for Experiencing Affection in Doings with Others* won sufficient votes to decide the issue.

It came as no surprise to Tucker that when the new catalogue of courses was printed for the incoming semester he learned that President Longshot had gotten Mildred Castleton to underwrite the Tittiley sisters' salaries by pointing out how much he knew she would want to support the seminary's teaching of "Do unto others as you would have them do unto you."

Episode 8

Star-Cross Seeks to Improve Town-Gown Relations

TOWN AND GOWN RELATIONS had never been strong since Star-Cross's reopening, and as the school now struggled to enhance its reputation in hopes of gaining enrollment the need had increasingly been felt to distinguish itself even further from its immediate environment. Most of the current faculty and students were not native to the area and at least unconsciously, it should be acknowledged, tended to view their location and neighbors with at least a benign cultural condescension. But what occasioned the latest conflict was a decision on the part of the local county executives to redraw the postal districts in the county with the consequence that new road signs and postal addresses would now be required.

For most of its existence Star-Cross had received its mail through general delivery from the local county post office zip code but in an effort to enhance its public image had unofficially inserted the words "Sacred Gardens" just before the county name on all its publications as if part of its proper address. With the redrawing of the postal districts this address addition would no longer be acceptable, and all of the seminary's periodicals and enrollment forms that carried the old address would have to be changed.

During the years that the Cross of Calvary Seminary had lain dormant the uninhabited area down hill from its campus had come to be used as the county dump and was even designated on the county maps as such. The Castleton Trust had initially persuaded the county to have the road that led into the seminary repaved, but there was little enthusiasm among the local politicians for spending tax money on a place that the locals mainly viewed with indifference, if not outright suspicion, and the road was not given a name. The result of this latest redistricting, however, had been that a new road sign and mail address box installed by the county at the entrance to the seminary now read *County Dump: Waste Management Site of Star-Cross Seminary.* When the seminary's outrage was expressed the local politicians simply replied that no discrediting was intended and that they were simply following the designations that had long appeared on the county maps. This had so infuriated President Longshot that he had sought once again the legal counsel of the Castleton Trust regarding the possibility of filing a suit against the county for defamation of school character and redress of grievances. How, he asked, could Star-Cross expect to enhance its national and, hopefully, even international reputation as a leading center of enlightened spirituality when all of its mail was being delivered to the postal address of *County Dump: Waste Management Site?*

Tucker had not been privy to this negotiation and did not know the extent to which Mildred Castleton herself had even been aware of it, but the Castleton Trust legal staff had managed to get the matter quietly resolved before the dispute with Longshot became public. The resulting accommodation, however, had only been the county's willingness to remove the seminary's name from the road sign and allow the seminary to construct a separate one for itself further up the road. Longshot clearly had not been satisfied by this less than ideal address change, but this time in a reverse set of circumstances Mildred's attorneys had enlisted Tucker to convince the president to lie low for the time being until more favorable public relations with the local residents and county politicians could be developed.

To that end Longshot had proposed a series of measures which in retrospect appeared to have had at best only a dubious effect. In one venture he had sent notices to the churches in the vicinity that Star-Cross would offer free *Hatha Yoga* meditation classes once a week for all their interested members to attend. Two of these invited congregations it turned out had fundamentalist pastors who regularly preached against yoga as paganism, one even characterizing the elitist liberals' preoccupation with such meditation techniques as a form of Satanism. The Roman Catholics in the area, whose prior contact with the seminary had mainly been over the suspicions surrounding the alleged mishandling of the endowment funds left by the disbanded convent of the Amazon Sisters of St. Fabula for the upkeep of her reliquary remains, never replied to the invitation. Two or three members of a small Episcopal parish where Tucker sometimes attended, signed up but later cancelled because of their inability, as they said, to commit to any regular schedule. And the remaining small Baptist, Methodist, and Presbyterian churches that eventually did reply to Longshot's letter simply observed in effect that their own weekly calendars of church activities did not have space for any more meetings.

A further attempt to develop better town/gown relations hardly proved more successful. In an effort to attract a wider range of interest, and one not simply focused upon the churches, with which Star-Cross frankly had little to do anyway, a widespread announcement was broadcast on the local radio that the seminary would host an afternoon of country music and free refreshments for all the family. When Tucker inquired of the President what "country music" group he had secured, Longshot seemed surprised by the question and said that he had asked Isadora Broadside to provide the music at the sacred gardens. Suspecting the worst mix up, and rightly so, Tucker checked with Professor Broadside and learned that she was indeed intending to do an Asian country lute recital with intermittent atonal chanting near the lotus plants harboring the Buddha statue.

By a last minute effort Tucker had managed to get several students to hook up some of the latest popular country music tapes available to a loud speaker on the far distant side of the campus and distribute the free ice cream and cake from there. The crowd had immediately gravitated from the Sacred Garden lute concert toward the more familiar steel guitar and banjo sounds and vocals of the country music tapes behind the refreshment stands, but fortunately Professor Broadside and her few devotees had remained so absorbed in their efforts that they appeared not to be aware of this dispersion.

Episode 9

Longshot's Quick Fix Plan to Give Free AAR Memberships to the Faculty

As THE TIME HAD drawn near for the renewal of the seminary's academic accreditation by the American Association of Theological Schools the apprehension had increased among the abler members of the Star-Cross faculty that the seminary as presently constituted might no longer be judged to meet the standards required by its visiting examiners. These examiners, as was the custom, consisted of four members chosen from faculties of other accredited seminaries throughout the country that had no previous ties to Star-Cross. Their professional assignment was to pay a three day visit to the campus for on-site inspection and interviews before offering their assessment and recommendations. The school's responsibility was to prepare beforehand a comprehensive self-study with statistical data for the committee to read in advance. As feared by the abler faculty, this initial visit had not gone well, and in Tucker's personal opinion it had proved a definite setback. The result was that Star-Cross had been put on notice that certain perceived weaknesses would have to be addressed before any renewal of its certification as an academically qualified seminary could be decided.

Four areas had been designated by the examiners as being most problematic and requiring immediate answers and clarification. The first had to do with finances, the second with a seeming lack of what the seminary understood its mission or sense of purpose to be, the third with what clearly appeared at least to be a decline across the board in curriculum requirements and faculty publishing, and the fourth questioned the job placements of its most recent graduates. The report specifically expressed astonishment at the fact that, with the exception of Tucker and only two other faculty, none of the fifteen or so other instructors currently offering courses at Star-Cross held membership, or ever had presented a paper, in the major professional organization for academics teaching in religious studies known as The American Academy of Religion.

In a three day series of meetings with the visiting committee Tucker had felt acute embarrassment at the school's poor showing and was relieved to have other faculty members take the lead in trying to make the most favorable case possible for the school's present situation. But now President Longshot had sought his counsel about how best to respond to the examiners' critical questions. Longshot had, in fact, so Tucker discovered upon his arrival at the president's office, already decided on a prepared set of explanations rebuffing each criticism. With a sense of self-satisfaction he presented them to Tucker to look over, not for advice, Tucker immediately realized, but for approval. They consisted basically of a whitewash of the school's problems, with imprecise assurances of exciting plans for the future to meet accreditation standards expressed in a series of euphemisms that left Tucker dumbfounded and wondering how Longshot could ever read them aloud without strangling.

Not waiting for a response, Longshot got to the point of why he had summoned Tucker. "What we need right away is a quick fix," he said, leaning across his desk with his finger jabbing the air. "Something to show these fossil bureaucrats that they are not going to get away with making bad publicity to destroy Star-Cross." The plan Longshot proposed was the following. The seminary would pay the membership and meeting fees yearly for every person on the faculty to become part, in Longshot's words, of "whatever the damn organization was that the report talked about." "The *AAR*," Tucker interjected, "*The American Academy of Religion*." "We'll have," Longshot continued, "a public ceremony with an invitation list of all members throughout the region who along with the press will be guests of the seminary to witness this event. I'll bet you," Longshot confided, "there is not a school anywhere around that can top the record of paying annually the total membership expenses for every single one of its faculty. Just think, Tucker, of the favorable publicity this will bring us, and how the accreditors' complaints will look then." Longshot then proceeded to explain to Tucker how he planned to present the request for the needed funds to Mildred Castleton and how confident he was that she would support the idea, even though, he acknowledged the plan would not be cheap. "I have already," Longshot concluded, "given my secretary the task of sending formal looking invitations to the entire membership list of all of this *AR*—or whatever you call it—organization from a hundred miles around. She will also order the membership cards for each of our faculty members, and we will invite Castleton on stage to congratulate each one as I present them. This event I tell you will surely make some headlines."

"What I need from you," Longshot continued with growing enthusiasm, "is for you to first present a short scholarly paper to set the tone of this assembly—something brief but technical enough to impress the audience of the school's scholarly credentials. Take that subject I recall you said you once debated at some conference about whether St. Paul's statement somewhere in the New Testament that `Christ is the *telos* of the Law' should be interpreted to read that `Christ is the *termination* of the Law' or that `Christ is the *fulfillment* of the Law.' Something vague like that, Tucker, really abstract but not too long, just to set a high intellectual tone. Frankly, of the two interpretations I don't care where you come down, just as long as you don't say anything controversial that will stir up all these academics or make too much of a difference."

Despite his most determined efforts Tucker in the following days had not been able to come up with any opening remarks as prescribed for such a befuddling occasion. To his overwhelming relief as circumstances developed, so it turned out, his inability did not matter. On the night of the big event observers immediately began to notice the demographics of the constituency arriving with their invitations to fill the hall where Mildred waited to be escorted into her position before the cameras. Many arrivals seemed to be her peers or even older, and a number were on walkers or in wheel chairs. Wondering what may have happened, but disbelieving that the president's secretary could have made such a stupendous mistake, Tucker hastened to ask to see the AAR membership cards from *The American Academy of Religion* the President was holding to present to the faculty members as they assembled on stage.

Incredibly, just as he realized what a calamitous mix-up was about to occur, a huge sign was brought out as the headline backdrop for all the news reporters to photograph, **FULL MEMBERSHIP GRANTED ALL STAR-CROSS SEMINARY FACULTY IN AARP—*THE AMERICAN ASSOCIATION OF RETIRED PERSONS.***

Episode 10

Star-Cross Struggles to Define its Mission: Angelica Visits Mildred

THE FINAL REPORT FROM the Association of Theological Schools accrediting committee following their on-sight visit to the seminary and their subsequent assessment of its overall situation had, as Tucker had feared, been severely critical. Star-Cross had been granted one year to get its house in order to demonstrate that the school had a clearly defined mission and knew what it was about. This censure had understandably not been well received by the President and most of the newer faculty who contended that the examining committee had definitely been weighted in the direction of more traditional conservatives. This increased the faculty tension between the more senior and the recently hired instructors, with each side tending to blame the other for the school's poor showing.

President Longshot, ever aware of Star-Cross's financial dependence upon the Castleton Trust, had become increasingly anxious that Mildred Castleton not learn of this humiliating report, most especially its major overall criticism that Star-Cross lacked a clear sense of mission. He had with impressive agility managed on the spur of the moment to cover up the earlier fiasco of the AAR membership cards by instantly recasting that occasion on the spot as actually a ceremony intended to honor all invited retirees in the audience, who without further ado had then been hustled to hastily set up tables of punch and cookies over which Mildred, still positioned in camera view, had been asked to give thanks. But Longshot was well aware that "mission" had been the defining term of identification in the former days when the old Cross of Calvary Seminary had been renowned for its training of missionaries and had proudly boasted of its missionary commitment in all its publications as "the proclamation of the Gospel to every living creature." It was obvious that Longshot's sympathies lay with those who thought that such an exclusivist Christian statement of mission, as they characterized it, did not represent the post-Christendom spirituality that a seminary today should be attuned to in a multi-religious and pluralistic world. Nevertheless, once again he had called upon Tucker to think up a way, before any news of the accreditation's report would leak out, to reassure their chief benefactor that Star-Cross remained staunchly faithful to its historic mission heritage.

Again this was no easy assignment, and for some days Tucker had worried over what he honestly could advise or do. It therefore came as a serendipitous gift when he received an email from a student requesting an appointment to meet with him to discuss, as she put it, her desire that the seminary remain committed spiritually to what she had thought it would, or should, be.

Angelica Blankchek introduced herself and thanked Tucker for taking the time to meet with her. She apologized that she had not yet had the privilege of taking any of his courses, which she heard were wonderful, but several of her friends had told her that she would find Prof. Schmoot sympathetic to her concerns. Tucker felt an instant rapport with the student, and when she told him that she had studied so far mainly with Isadora Broadside, with the addition of one course taught by the Tittiley sisters that had a title she could not recall, he was certain that their dissatisfactions over the current dismissal of Star-Cross's Reformed biblical heritage would be tending in the same direction.

Angelica was clearly intelligent and spoke with appealing conviction. "I am worried, Professor Schmoot, that we may be in danger of forgetting our spiritual purpose today as a seminary. I don't mean to complain or sound overly dramatic, and maybe others feel differently, but I just wonder, for all our talk about inclusiveness, if Star-Cross is really addressing the spiritual needs of our time."

"Yes, yes, I hear you," Tucker had replied reassuringly, trying not to reveal how much he agreed with her sentiments. Inquiry into anyone's personal faith was strictly taboo at Star-Cross, but Tucker surmised where Angelica was coming from, and he could hardly contain his satisfaction that there were still students around unafraid to go against the stream in standing up for their beliefs. Their conversation had continued through much of the lunch hour, and with increasing confidence Tucker suddenly realized that the fervent Miss Blankchek would be the ideal one to assure Mildred Castleton that faith commitment and a sense of mission were not lacking among Star-Cross students. When Tucker asked Angelica if she would be willing to share her very important and, in his considered judgment, well founded insights with one of the seminary's chief supporters, the young woman eagerly agreed, and when an acceptable time had been arranged they were cordially greeted at the Castleton homeplace as they arrived for afternoon tea.

Tucker observed with admiration Angelica's courtesy in expressing appreciation for Mildred Castleton's warm welcome and noted to his satisfaction that Mildred in turn seemed pleased to meet such an attractive student from the seminary. "Tell me about your seminary experience," Mildred had inquired with genuine interest.

"To be honest," Angelica responded, "I am concerned that Star-Cross not lose its purpose of recognizing what the spiritual needs of today are. And I care about this because Star-Cross is about the only seminary around that claims to take seriously that we live in a pluralistic age of many spiritual varieties called by many different names with many so-called sacred scriptures that are often used to assert their authority as if their way is the only way and discredit one another in a manner that is not accepting of all. Mrs. Castleton, I hate to have to say it, but at Star-Cross today the increasing number of incoming students who spiritually do not identify as theists are sometimes not given the respect they deserve, especially by the more traditional faculty. It is a subtle discrimination, like that toward women who try to raise a critical voice. No one explicitly admits to it. But if you don't fit into some mainstream religious box, as I do not, you are made aware, despite what the Star-Cross catalogue says, of being viewed as somehow spiritually lacking and inferior. We are not like the fundamentalists, but frankly I am afraid we are going to start attracting students who are. We still have stained glass windows of mostly male religious figures," Angelica continued, "and another thing—I have counted a number of crosses in the stone masonry of our buildings, quite a few, even though they try to cover them up with ivy and shrubbery and the lotus plants in the Sacred Garden, but do you know that there is not one star anywhere on our buildings? Not one, and we claim to be spiritually open to an ever expanding interstellar universe beyond traditional religion and call ourselves *Star*-Cross Spirituality Seminary."

Angelica's recital, to Tucker's confounding, continued in this unexpected manner despite his futile attempts to intervene and change the subject. Mildred had listened respectfully and given Angelica her full attention. As soon as possible Tucker arranged for their departure with effusive thanks to Mildred for her hospitality and assurance that they would be in touch. Angelica expressed her pleasure in being able to share her concerns and remained blissfully unaware that she had torpedoed Tucker's primary aim in introducing her to the seminary's dear benefactor. Tucker dreaded what he would have to report to Longshot, or how he could explain what had happened at tea.

After driving Angelica back to campus, he had ridden alone in the setting sun along the back country roads that were his refuge when he most needed time to think. The hour was late when he returned, tired and still chagrinned by his own miscalculations. He almost put off checking his messages until the morning, but when he saw one from Mildred Castleton, texted to him by a secretary of the Castleton Trust, he opened it with uneasiness and began to read:

> Dear Professor Schmoot,
>
> You are indeed so kind to allow me the pleasure of meeting members of our current seminary student body. I always find these cherished occasions such food for my soul. Did you notice dear Angelica's passion and commitment? It was so encouraging for me to listen to her, and it recalled the urgency of my own years in the World Student Christian Federation when I was her age and our slogan then was "The World for Christ in One Generation." Our way of expressing ourselves may change, but the mission remains. How grateful I am to be able to do whatever I can for a student generation such as this. You must be so proud.
>
> Thank you again for keeping me informed.
>
> Mildred Castleton

Episode 11

Outside Consultant Speaks to Faculty on Academic Assessment

ATTEMPTS TO AGREE ON a grading system at Star-Cross had divided the faculty since the beginning, but now that the accrediting committee of the American Association of Theological Schools had mandated that the seminary clarify its reason for being and specify its academic standards, some decision could no longer be avoided.

An initial effort by President Longshot to get the faculty on its own to solve the problem wasted several months of meeting time that amounted to an exercise in futility. Each of the four curricular areas traditionally designated in most seminaries since the nineteenth century simply as Bible, Church History, Systematic Theology, and Practice of Ministry—and now progressively renamed at Star-Cross in keeping with its postmodern suspicions of authoritarianism as, for Bible, *Comparative Hegemonics*, for Church History, *Deconstructive History*, for Systematic Theology, *Spiritual Psychology*, and for Practice of Ministry, *Experiential Modalities and Practices*—had argued for its own proposals but could elicit no agreement from the others.

The once Bible faculty, of which Tucker was a mostly silent New Testament member whose generally repressed disagreements on such contentious issues had long since let the more outspoken have their say, had insisted that students in their courses should not be required to know scriptural content in any factual sense, which they associated with fundamentalist scripture quoting, but rather should be judged on how creatively they were able to pick out those parts of scripture that tended to support their personal interests and values today.

The historians argued, somewhat similarly, for examining their student's ability to suspect whose narrative is shaping the so-called "history" under consideration and whose social interests this narrative really serves.

The representatives of theology, on the other hand, passionately objected to text based learning and insisted that in spiritual contexts student accomplishments were most aptly judged by some performance as in the arts. When dance, for example, becomes the approved medium for a final evaluation in systematic theology rather than a written exam or research term paper, the criterion of "balance," they explained, takes center stage as never before. When asked how anyone could ever fail such an exam, it was admitted that at least one student a few years earlier because of a severe weight problem and an overly constricted leotard had indeed lost balance and fallen over a chair, requiring an exam retake with a much less strenuous lute accompaniment at a later date.

For their part the instructors in Experiential Modalities and Practices advocated their standard of evaluation simply as what works best—and apparently became confused when asked, "Best for whom?"

It was against this background that President Longshot resolved without further delay to take matters into his own hands and announced that he had hired a renowned outside consultant to mentor and oversee the implementation of an academic assessment policy at Star-Cross. The individual he had selected, so the faculty was informed with some swagger, was a reputedly distinguished international director of the *Center for Religious*

Assessment Policies, or CRAP, Tucker thought to himself, according to its acronym. Longshot did not divulge that he had only learned of the consultant from Wisteria Dean who had boasted of having worked with the academic celebrity.

Not knowing what to expect, but not being in any position in their irritation for not having been consulted to raise objections, the faculty grudgingly assembled at the appointed time for their initial encounter with the outside consultant. Waiting to begin, Tucker reflected how outside consultants are probably among the least welcome people in any organization. In this instance, the visitor, who asked to be called simply Brother John, arrived dressed in what appeared to be a combination of a dashiki and a saffron monk's robe with prayer shawl and embroidered stole and wearing a colorful turban for his introductory presentation. The attempt was obviously to appear trans-spiritually inclusive, Tucker thought, though no one of any particular religious tradition would likely identify with such a garb. He later learned that Brother John had grown up a born-again Baptist in Topeka.

After a fulsome introduction by Longshot, the lecturer outlined his subject and presentation. He would address the faculty on the theme of *Fingering Our Spiritual Pulse,* a topic, Tucker suspected, that was the speaker's well rehearsed stock in trade. It consisted of three parts, as Tucker would try later to recall. First point: "fingering," which was elaborated tediously in more than sufficient detail to stress a "hands on approach" to the subject matter. Second point: "spiritual," interpreted vaguely as anything ultimately intangible connected to the soul, which clearly, if intangible, invalidated the first point and any possibility of fingering. And third, "pulse": which was explained as providing the three most basic questions in a policy of spiritual assessment: (1) Is the pulse too slow to *sustain* life?, (2) Is it too erratic to *obtain* consistency?, and (3) Is the pulse too rapid to *retain* vitality?

All around him Tucker could sense a growing restlessness in the room, though a few, as always, dutifully continued to take notes throughout the hour. Tucker especially was struck by Isadora Broadside's gleaming approval. His colleague was clearly taken by the representative from CRAP, and Tucker was immediately ashamed of himself for imagining what perhaps the faculty's most self-assured paragon of spirituality would do if she should ever get the outside consultant into the Sacred Garden. President Longshot beamed with satisfaction as well, oblivious as usual to the prevailing mood around him.

A recess was called with the faculty asked to return in thirty minutes without Brother John present to affirm their support of his mentorship. When most of them had reassembled the opposition was apparent, and Longshot appeared stunned that his choice of an outside consultant had not met with enthusiastic approval. "I have already obtained substantial funds from the Castleton Trust to underwrite his services," he pleaded with exasperation, which only further inflamed the disapproving faculty. As other faculty members were entering the room Longshot continued demanding, "Why is this consultant not suitable? Why is his policy of 'fingering our spiritual pulse' not what we need? Why? Just give me one reason, why?"

"Because," suddenly sounded the outraged voice of a very red faced Isadora Broadside just coming through the door, "That's not all he's fingering!"

And with that the meeting abruptly adjourned.

Episode 12

Longshot Proposes Distinguished Spirits Professorships

WITH THE FACULTY'S INABILITY to agree on a grading system, and its rejection of the President's choice of an outside consultant to assist the seminary in evaluating its purpose and programs, as the accrediting committee's rules for all theological schools required, Longshot postponed these matters. At least for the time being, he decided to turn his attention to a more achievable goal – namely, that of improving morale among both his teachers and the student body. He announced a ten percent increase in all faculty salaries, beginning immediately, and advised the student body that a moratorium on all grading would be in effect for the current academic year. These decisions, as expected, brought a sharp rise in the administration's overall favorability ratings, and effectively eliminated for the moment all dissent.

To get around the accreditation requirements, so he confided to Tucker, he had devised an "end run idea," as he put it, that would guarantee Star-Cross's reputation as a first rate institution, regardless of the accrediting bureaucrats. The seminary would begin awarding honorary doctoral degrees to famous individuals and name them as Distinguished Spiritual Professors of faculty chairs at Star-Cross.

When Tucker asked what "famous individuals" he had in mind, Longshot with a wink and a confident smile said, "That's the genius of my idea, Tucker. These will all be posthumous. World class figures like Mahatma Gandhi, Nelson Mandela, Mother Theresa—you get the point, Tucker?—and in time, the Dali Lama. Now that would be a winner! Just imagine how our faculty roster would look with Distinguished Professor Gandhi at Star-Cross, Distinguished Professor Mandela at Star-Cross, Distinguished Professor Mother Theresa at Star-Cross, et cetera, et cetera. The possibilities are endless. No school could top that, right?"

"But, I guess I don't understand how posthumous professorships would work," Tucker said, trying not to show how appalling he found such a proposal. "I can see naming faculty chairs in memory of some outstanding individuals after their death, but I don't know what it would mean to list them as current faculty. I am afraid I don't get it."

"But that's what I want you to get," Longshot responded directly. "Try thinking outside the box. We are a non-traditional center of spirituality. Spirituality is our trademark, and it is the coming thing today. By appointing posthumous Distinguished Spiritual Professorships we are publicizing that the *spirit* of each of these individuals is alive in our curriculum. What I want you to do," Longshot looked at Tucker with determination, "is to prepare me a list of world famous inspirational figures we could select from and advertise how their spirit best correlates with Star-Cross's current curriculum. Hell, I'm not asking that you make Broadside into Mother Theresa, or the Dali Lama (she'd prefer that, if he were a candidate!)—no sexist or gender identifications—we need to be beyond all that. What I am asking is that you draw up a proposal for me about which professorships should carry which names, so that I can make these awards and appointments. Understand?"

"Just one thing further," Longshot added, "Don't let any of the faculty know whose positions are going to be named distinguished professorships, and don't pick any names that Mildred Castleton might disapprove of."

Tucker had remained respectful of the President's suggestions in his meeting with Longshot, as was his manner, but he knew nothing would come of such a strange idea of naming posthumous professorships and in fact, as he suspected, nothing did. He had in good conscience quietly broached the subject to several of his trusted faculty colleagues, who with less charity in their response had found the whole proposal hilarious. He also did his best to come up with a list of spiritually inspiring famous names, as the President had requested, but none met with sufficient support or agreement from either the faculty or students to form a consensus when he merely mentioned them in casual conversation, without, of course, divulging why: Dag Hammarskjöld, the Swedish Secretary General of the United Nations (1953–61), killed in an African plane crash, who left behind his inspirational *Markings*; Sakakawea, the Native American girl guide of the Lewis and Clark Expedition; Kahlil Gibran, the mystically romantic Lebanese poet and best selling author of *The Prophet*, a favored read at nontraditional weddings. These three came closest to being unobjectionable, but three were hardly enough for a list, and Tucker thought it better not to pursue it. To Tucker's relief, Longshot soon had become distracted with other matters, as was often the case, and did not contact him further about his Distinguished Spirits professorial proposal.

Episode 13

Tucker's Advice Sought by Junior Colleague

WITH THE REQUIREMENT NOW mandated for Star-Cross to clarify its institutional identity as a seminary and demonstrate its academic credentials Tucker had turned his attention to his own area of biblical scholarship and more specifically to the curriculum of what had once been called New Testament studies. Besides himself, only one of his New Testament colleagues in the renamed department of *Comparative Hegemonics* currently had a book in publication, a largely conventional restatement of arguments against the authority of scripture titled *Who's to Say?* In his own case Tucker himself was not without occasional feelings of dissatisfaction for his own conformity in avoiding all personal faith statements in his academic publications by addressing the content of the New Testament writings only obliquely through such noncommittal subjects as *Parallels in Sacred Writings*.

The insistence of the administration that all faculty appointees enhance Star-Cross's reputation by producing books in keeping with the nonexclusive spirituality of the seminary had prompted an urgent request to Tucker from a younger member in his department seeking his advice regarding a manuscript on which the young colleague was working. Batson Belfry had grown up in an evangelical family in central Oklahoma where both of his parents were preachers, and he had written a dissertation in a conservative seminary on a standard doctrinal subject of *Christology and Revelation.* In Tucker's estimation the young man nevertheless was exceptionally bright, and for this dissertation he had received high marks and recommendations that had gotten him an entering trial position at Star-Cross, not his first choice, but a needed job where the opportunities were few. Tucker had become impressed by the hard working intelligence of this unlikely New Testament assistant at a place like Star-Cross, and when Batson asked his advice regarding publication he was willing to do what he could to be of help.

The manuscript, Batson acknowledged, that he was asking Tucker to look at was basically a rewritten version of his doctoral dissertation which he was attempting to cast in a new key more in tune with the marketing requirements of Star-Cross. Several prospective publishers whom the administration had recommended he consult had rejected his original dissertation subject as "boringly traditional," but one had advised that he consider changing it to something "with a catchy title." Batson, after discussing this prospect with some of the students at Star-Cross who proved largely unfamiliar with such terms as *Christology* and *Revelation* had agreed that he needed a "catchier" subject, and he wondered if Tucker thought a book on *Jesus As God's Selfie*, a statement he had seen on a church billboard, would sound scholarly enough.

He then proceeded to outline for Tucker the table of contents as he had been trying to re-envision it. Chapter 1 of *Jesus as God's Selfie* would be titled "Who Is In The Picture?" Chapter 2 would be, "Who Is Holding The Camera?" Chapter 3 then would follow with, "Who Makes The Click?"

As Batson laid out his proposal, Tucker was heartened by his young colleague's earnestness and ingenuity. There was something authentic about Batson's commitment to his project, though Tucker was not sure how to judge it. "I won't testify to any of my own faith about these three questions," Batson continued, "if you agree that, career wise, it would be better for me as an academic not to take an explicit Christian position here at Star-Cross. Instead, I'll simply set forth the religious issues objectively in terms of their pros and cons without divulging any personal faith commitments. If I stay noncommittal about my own beliefs, and not come across as an Okie zipper-Bible thumper, would that not give me a better chance of getting published in a way more consistent with the image Star-Cross wants to project?"

Batson paused and looked expectantly at Tucker for a reply. For an instant Tucker was caught off guard by his young colleague's apparent trust in his judgment. His own vocational commitments dormant from an earlier day flashed uninvited through his mind. Resistant to being cast too enthusiastically in the uncomfortable role of a mentor, Tucker heard himself responding in the most neutral voice he could muster, "Perhaps we could meet again when we've had more time to think about this further."

Episode 14

Longshot's Deceptive Faculty Christmas Party

BECAUSE OF THE END of the fall term responsibilities, Batson and Tucker had only had time to greet each other in passing, but with the coming Christmas season they had agreed to meet again for a further conversation after the students had left on their holiday break. The most convenient occasion, they decided, would be the holiday party for the faculty that President Longshot hosted every year which was without a doubt the one moment of his greatest annual popularity. Only Tucker was aware—and this even he had not discovered until the last year or so—that the lavish outlay of this supposed presidential generosity was but another example of presidential duplicity. Every individual on the faculty and administrative staff was customarily given the choice of a bottle of vintage wine or of nonalcoholic cider, along with a colorfully arranged basket of gourmet chocolates, richly decorated cookies and pastries, a smoked turkey and baked ham, tins of imported caviar, and an assortment of the finest fruits and cheeses. This occasion was no doubt the single event approaching even a semblance of good cheer that one could find all year long at Star-Cross where relations between the faculty and the administration, to put it mildly,

were far from harmonious. Typically, as soon as Longshot presented the baskets and bottles as his personal presidential gifts most of
the faculty members would cart their booty away, sometimes even
before the President had finished giving his brief holiday greet-
ings and remarks. What Tucker had quite unexpectedly discovered
only two years previously was that all this holiday largesse did not
in fact come from Longshot himself but was instead his deliberately misrepresented gifts for the faculty and staff that Mildred
Castleton herself had provided to the seminary every Christmas
season, personally making sure that every faculty or staff name
was inscribed on one of the baskets and bottles. Only by accident
did Tucker happen one year to see workers across campus unload-
ing the Castleton Chrysler that Clarence had driven to the back
door of the President's office. As usual, Tucker had kept Longshot's
hoax to himself, not mentioning it to anyone, and concealing
his feelings of guilt that no one ever thanked Mildred Castleton
herself for her generosity in actually being the one responsible for
their holiday party.

As he was sitting and talking with Batson while waiting for the
annual all-holidays distribution to begin, Tucker noticed a highly
agitated Longshot conferring at the door with several of his staff.
Instead of the usual cart loads of gifts, they handed the President
only a single box containing an envelope for each faculty member.
Appearing uncertain himself as to what to do with the envelopes,
Longshot hurriedly placed the box by the exit and disappeared,
leaving his staff to explain that there had been some delay in the
President's gift orders this year which he had gone to investigate.
Instead, everyone was urged to take his or her addressed envelope
as they left. Tucker and Batson waited in line to get theirs, and this
is what they read:

> Dear Star-Cross Faculty and Staff,
>
> For many years, as you who have been here awhile know,
> it has been my great pleasure to provide for your Christ-
> mas Party with gifts that hopefully you could share with
> your families and loved ones at this Holy Season. This
> year all of us are aware, I am sure, of so much suffering

in the world that I knew you would agree with me that our gifts should go to those less fortunate. Therefore, I have sent in your name checks to the *Children's Refugee Assistance Program.* This idea was proposed to me just recently and most urgently by your beloved former dean, Dr. Wisteria Dean, who writes that she is currently in charge of refugee missions in troubled areas of this world. Let us pray that by sending our monetary contributions to her the light of Star-Cross this year will shine in the darkness.

May God bless you, one and all, in this Christmas season of our Savior's birth.

Sincerely, in His name and in yours,

Mildred Castleton

Episode 15

Batson Expresses a Vocational Interest in Mission Work

BATSON AND TUCKER CONTINUED to confer about publishing matters following the miscarriage of the President's holiday party. Since Batson had not yet joined the faculty when Wisteria Dean had briefly been in charge of the administrative office during President Longshot's earlier sabbatical, he knew nothing of the questionable mismanagement that had led to her dismissal. In this respect, Tucker realized with concern that Batson was as unaware of all this as was apparently Mildred Castleton herself. On that previous occasion Longshot had indeed managed to keep the whole matter hushed up and prevent a damaging scandal from becoming public. This time, once again, the faculty remained similarly indifferent to the whole anomaly and simply dismissed it as typical of the President's seeming inability to get anything right.

Tucker himself, however, remained disturbed by Mildred Castleton's reference to having received a solicitation from Wisteria Dean and first sought information from Longshot who abruptly dismissed his inquiry by saying there had just been some misunderstanding which his office had taken care of. Not wishing to venture into administrative matters between the President's office and the Castleton Trust that were none of his business, but still concerned, Tucker in his thank-you note to the dear lady commending her generous Christmas contributions in the faculty's name to aid refugee children had simply, off-handedly, expressed wonder about Wisteria Dean's current address for receiving funds. Shortly thereafter, he had received a reply that they were wired simply according to Dean's instructions to the *Committee on Refugee Assistance Program* at a post office box address in Atlanta, and marked for overseas forwarding. There was a postscript in Mildred Castleton's handwritten reply thanking Tucker most heartily for his personal interest in supporting Dr. Dean's missionary activities.

For the remainder of the holiday season Tucker was preoccupied with other activities that prevented his pursuing the question of the refugee contributions further. But soon after classes resumed a most unexpected development occurred in his meetings with Batson. The young man reported that after working almost nonstop on the rewrite of his dissertation on *Christology and Revelation* under the new, hopefully catchier title of *Jesus as God's Selfie*, he was having a troubled conscience about the whole enterprise of simply trying to earn professional advancement as a biblical scholar by such disingenuous means. He confided in Tucker, whose understanding he clearly relied on, that he wanted a more faithful purpose in his life, whether or not he was able to stay at Star-Cross beyond his entering trial position, or ever manage to find another academic position elsewhere. "I can't pretend I am not who I am," he said. Then, with both of them feeling somewhat embarrassed by such confessional frankness, he added, "I guess I really do care about the Gospel."

"Have you considered going into the ministry?," Tucker asked, "or speaking with your church about ordination?"

"I'm not sure where I belong denominationally," Batson acknowledged, "but for the moment I am thinking of exploring the possibility of some short term mission work, something perhaps as a back up to my teaching here, in case my contract is not renewed next year. The idea came to me with the letters we received at the President's holiday party. I wrote and thanked the lady who sent them for making the contributions to the refugee children on our behalf instead of spending so much on gifts for us this year, and I asked her how to get in touch with this mission as I would like to be part of it."

"What did she say?," Tucker asked.

"Oh, she encouraged me to write to the post office box of a *Committee on Refugee Assistance Program* that is located in Atlanta, and she even offered to pay my air fare if I wanted to make a quick trip appointment for an interview. Isn't that amazing, almost like providence, isn't it?"

"Are you going to follow up?," Tucker responded.

"I already have, that's what I've been wanting to tell you. I managed to contact this address about an interview, not mentioning my present position. The reply I got back from Atlanta was a solicitation for a further contribution to the *Committee on Refugee Assistance Program* to be made out simply to the initials C-R-A-P. It was signed by the managing director in charge who goes by his monastic name of `Brother John.'"

Faced with Batson's enthusiasm Tucker managed to conceal his alarm at suddenly realizing that his unsuspecting young colleague as well as their benefactor was at risk of falling prey to a most likely scam. To avoid overreacting, and yet forestall any sudden actions on Batson's part, he simply suggested casually that perhaps it might be better if Batson postponed all further contacts with the Atlanta mission until after the forthcoming proposals for an updated Star-Cross Handbook of seminary policy and practices were scheduled to be voted on. Batson had readily agreed and again thanked Tucker who parted hoping that this play for time would, at least in the interim, avert what could well become a crisis of the most entangling complications.

Episode 16

Faculty Settles on Pan-Pneumatic to Characterize its Non-exclusivist Identity

THE PRODUCTION OF A Handbook of Star-Cross's governing policies had been in the works for some time. Attorneys for the seminary had warned that it was a legal requirement for the protection of all contracts, and at their insistence President Longshot had reluctantly appointed a drafting committee of representatives selected from the four departments of the curriculum to advise him in the writing. Not surprisingly, from the start disputes had arisen over the basis for any power of authorization in an institution supposedly committed to a non-authoritarian spirituality. With every idea from one group countered by objections from another, and with little prospect of an eventual consensus, the proposed document submitted for faculty vote had been reduced to a maximum vagueness. Tucker was thankful not to be involved, but he knew that one section to be proposed would address the question of faculty members' taking additional jobs outside the seminary, and it was this section that he feared might jeopardize Batson's position. In quickly reviewing the final draft distributed just before a faculty vote was scheduled to be taken, Tucker was relieved, even if a bit amused, to see that the outside employment stipulation had been left by the drafting committee as ambiguous as possible: *"No full time faculty member under the employ of the seminary shall accept additional outside hire in any capacity incommensurate with the seminary itself."* This deliberately innocuous wording, leaving "incommensurate" unspecified and thus unenforceable, no doubt reflected the ingenuity of the exhausted faculty representatives on the drafting committee eager to bring their unresolved disputes finally to their most watered down conclusion. Even so, President Longshot had been instructed by the seminary lawyers to add a clarifying addendum after full faculty consideration and approval stating what the majority opinion was of how the seminary was most properly to be characterized.

In the two hours of additional comment provoked by this addendum request five options for defining "spiritual commensurability" had been advocated by the faculty members without coming to agreement. The seminary Handbook would simply list them as follows:

(1) *Inter-religious.* Here objections were made that spirituality is not confined to religion in which the term "inter" connotes essentialist differentiations.

(2) This was thus changed to *Inter-faith* which the theological, or now Spiritual Psychology, instructors reminded their colleagues excludes from consideration the validity of those who, rightly or wrongly, claim not to have faith.

(3) The proposal was then offered that, rather than "inter," the term "trans" was more spiritually appropriate to name Star-Cross's inclusive identity as a seminary that was *Trans-spiritual*, a label promptly rejected by the historians as too easily confused with an un-deconstructed nineteenth century movement known as New England Transcendentalism.

(4) With this objection several others agreed and proposed *Trans-psychic* as a possible alternative. Quite understandably, such a characterization immediately occasioned the rebuke of

still others with the criticism that such a term failed to respect the bodily, and not simply the psychic, integrity of the transgendered.

(5) As the hour for adjournment approached with as yet no agreement, the futile attempt to characterize the inclusive spirituality commensurate with Star-Cross dropped both the prefixes "inter" and "trans" and settled instead on the Greek neologism *Pan-Pneumatic*. When the legal advisors asked for further definition of this term, a faculty consensus decidedly did emerge, in the words of one member, that they should "go look it up."

Episode 17

Librarian Raises Suspicions of Faculty-Student Misconduct

BECAUSE OF TIME CONSTRAINTS a related stipulation in a further section of the proposed Handbook on the propriety of faculty/student social relationships outside the classroom, i.e. dating, within such an all inclusive *Pan-Pneumatic* environment, had been passed over without comment. It read, "*While non-discriminatory supportive associations are permitted where power differentials between faculty and students are not involved, all teacher/student associative boundaries that give evidence of hetero-privileging should be avoided as incommensurate with relationships at Star-Cross.*" Protesting this oversight, and intimating suspicions that this ruling was currently being violated, Isadora Broadside insisted that before agreeing to an adjournment motion the faculty should amend it to resume their incomplete consideration of the Handbook the following day. And Longshot, fearing Broadside's displeasure more than the barely disguised sighs of resentment around the room, announced his presidential agreement that this would indeed be the case.

By the time for reconvening the next day it had became clear that the suspicions to which Isadora Broadside had alluded regarding possible faculty/student improprieties had come from

Star-Cross's recently hired director of the seminary library. Rigore Mortisse, who was but the latest in a series of rapidly changing librarians to occupy that post, was not as rigid and unbending as his unfortunate name suggested to some, but he had quickly established a stern reputation for asserting his authority in enforcing the library's rules. One of these was the absolute quiet demanded not only in the reading room but throughout the library. On several occasions in making his rounds Mortisse claimed to have spotted what he suspected to be one of Star-Cross's junior male instructors with a slightly younger female student huddled together in an out of the way alcove whispering over a reference volume which caused him to suspect that the couple's interests involved more than academic research. This suspicion was further confirmed to his consternation by checking the volume after they had departed and, lo and behold, discovering that it was an archival copy of the ancient graphic manual of Hindu eroticism, the *Kama Sutra*. Not knowing either of the individuals but determined to report the incident to the proper authorities, Mortisse had later expressed his concerns to Professor Broadside in passing, without going into details or mentioning specifics, and she had advised him to inform President Longshot right away.

Tucker had received a heads-up from Longshot the night before that a delicate matter might be coming up when the faculty reconvened the next day to consider the proposed Handbook stipulation regarding proper faculty/student social conduct, and he requested Tucker's support in keeping matters from getting out of hand. He said that Rigore Mortisse had related to him some very imprecise and unconfirmed information suggesting an improper liaison apparently between one of Star-Cross's male faculty members and a woman student. Since Mortisse had not known the name of either, Longshot said he had told the librarian that his suspicion was not enough to go on and that without further evidence the matter would not be brought up in the meeting. With that, Longshot told Tucker, he hoped that he had put a definite halt to any rumors from either Mortisse or Broadside.

Upon arriving for the meeting, however, Tucker confronted a very grim faced Longshot at the door. Motioning Tucker aside, the President confided to him that Mortisse had been so personally offended by what he viewed as a rejection of his integrity by Longshot's dismissal of his report that he had subsequently produced further evidence. When leaving campus the previous day at the close of the library Mortisse informed Longshot that he had recognized the same couple in a car together drive out of the parking lot, and he had followed at a distance to see where they were going. Sure enough, he had told Longshot, they had driven out of town into the country. When they turned off the main highway onto a narrower tree shrouded road Mortisse said he had lost sight of the car, but with confidence he provided Longshot with the route number that was posted at the turn-off.

"So, what was it?," Tucker asked, annoyed at even hearing of such snooping. When Longshot told him, the irony of the news of such a fools errand convulsed him. "Oh please, Mr. President," he responded, "you do realize that's the private road into Mildred Castleton's."

Episode 18

Batson Shares Self Doubts with Tucker over his Advisement of Angelica

LONGSHOT HAD MANAGED TO soothe Mortisse's offended feelings before calling the reconvened faculty to order. With assurance that his "see something, report something" suspicions would definitely be given, in Longshot's words, "the attention they deserved," the mollified librarian had agreed that such an investigative matter in principle should best be kept confidential and not brought up in an open meeting.

The new Handbook provision having to do with the propriety of faculty and student social relationships outside of class was readily accepted without objection and formally approved after only a few questions of clarification pertaining to the legalese of its framers' wording. As soon as the required final overall vote could be taken to approve the entire new Handbook, the faculty as if by bell had scrambled to adjourn and rapidly scatter before the scrutinizing legal advisers, whose job continuance depended upon their being so, could think up still further items requiring more time for additional deliberation and forestalling any conclusion.

Walking back across campus to his office, Tucker felt gratified that a seminary policy on social relationships at Star-Cross could be agreed upon so easily without controversy. Respect for diversity and personal privacy was one of the hallmarks of Star-Cross's live and let live atmosphere that he most valued. Having suffered the painful failure of an early marriage at the start of his career, for which he had never ceased feeling the blame for his academic preoccupations, Tucker had remained single and was glad for the non-inquisitive freedoms and supportive friendships across differences that life at Star-Cross provided. Mortisse's reported watch dogging he resented as an invasive proclivity for suspicion that violated the character of the place.

Almost as an illustration of his thoughts a friendly voice suddenly called out to him from a passing group of students. Turning around he was warmly greeted by Angelica Blankchek who expressed her eagerness to tell him about her recent invitation to speak to a church group at Mildred Castleton's. "It was to an Adult Bible Fellowship meeting in her home," Angelica explained. "She asked if I would just speak informally about my studies at Star-Cross. Isn't that incredible? I am not a church person, and the only thing I know about the Bible is what I am presently learning from Dr. Belfry in his introductory Comparative Hegemonics class. But, when I asked if he would help me adapt some of my ideas from an earlier research project for another class that's the main work I've done, he agreed, and, would you believe it, he was so interested to support me, Professor Schmoot, that he even went with me."

"Of course, I'd be happy to meet and hear more," Tucker said, to Angelica's delight. "Let me get in touch with Dr. Belfry, and we'll see what the best time would be for the three of us to get together."

Tucker had planned to contact Batson further as soon as the new Handbook proposals had been adopted to consider with him the possible risk to his faculty appointment at Star-Cross if he undertook additional part time mission work with the so-called *Committee on Refugee Assistance Program*, or whatever name the outfit went by, headed by Brother John in apparent league with Wisteria Dean that he suspected was scheming to milk the Castleton Trust from Atlanta. The unexpected campus encounter with Angelica Blankchek now provided him an extra incentive to do so without delay. But as he quickened his step, suddenly intrigued by the thought of finding out what all was really going on with his friend Batson, Tucker cautioned himself not to become as suspicious a snoop as poor Mortisse. In fact, he decided he would first wait to hear from his young colleague before reaching out to him on any matters himself. "What a day," Tucker chuckled to himself, as he opened the door to his office.

The wait would not be long, however, for when he picked up the note that had been slipped under his office door Tucker found an urgent appeal from Batson, asking if he could get his scholarly advice on a serious academic matter that greatly concerned him, but which he did not want to discuss in e-mails. Not knowing what exactly to expect, Tucker phoned Batson that he was welcome to come by his office as soon as convenient, and within the hour Batson arrived clearly worried about something.

One of the students in his introductory class, Batson explained, had asked him to take a look at a term paper she had earlier written as a research project in another course. She said that she had been requested by a church group in the area to speak about her seminary studies at Star-Cross and wondered if he would help her adapt some ideas from her research in preparing her presentation. He had agreed, but at first glance had been disturbed by the paper's title and the question of its suitability as an acceptable subject proper for a seminary. His problem, however, for which he now sought Tucker's counsel, was not that his initial objections had subsequently been confirmed. Quite to the contrary, he had in reading been so impressed with the quality of the student's insights that he had agreed to help her restate her ideas in a more biblical idiom. It was this agreement that he now regretted for having resulted in a recent situation in which he felt he had proven untrustworthy. Batson paused, unaware of the conversation that Tucker had just had with Angelica Blankchek, or of the library gossip from Rigore Mortisse that Longshot had informed Tucker about.

"What was the subject of the project?," Tucker asked.

"It was titled *The Spiritual Significance of Anti-Normativity in Ancient Hindu Eroticism*," Batson replied. "I know it sounds weird at first, and frankly ancient hieroglyphics are no great interest of mine, whether allegedly erotic or not. Since the student—Angelica Blankchek, whom I think you may know—claims that she never has had any experience with the Bible or the church, I just assumed that her project most probably would be another example of the sort of superficial New Age thinking and pagan infatuation that a lot of our students who have no background in traditional Christianity bring to this seminary.

But when I read it, Tucker, man was I mistaken! Her main thesis, to put it most succinctly, is that what a tradition portrays as abnormal, or contrary to the norm, may actually have the spiritual significance of opening that tradition to a deeper truth regarding its norm and the love it entails. Her scholarship is impeccable, and I have not seen a more profoundly argued paper from any student. Talk about Revelation and Christology! Tucker, she gets it, even though she doesn't know that's what she's talking about! My mistake was that I should never have encouraged her to try and recast her ideas in a biblical idiom to make them sound more acceptable to a church audience. I knew her social concern was to address the discrimination in what she considers to be the human rights abuses of sexual minorities today. But I also knew from my experiences with church people back home that this would not be a concern most of them would approve of as a topic for discussion in a Bible study group. So what I did was try to explain how Jesus taught in parables and was himself condemned for associating with outcasts, and that the Bible, contrary to what many of its defamers say, is not against sexual love, as the *Song of Songs* shows, but recognizes, to use Paul's terms, that not all *epithumia*, or passion, is *porneia*. Right?"

"So what is it that upsets you?," Tucker asked.

"It's that the Bible Fellowship Group where she spoke met at Mrs. Castleton's," Batson continued, "and I went along actually to help prevent misunderstanding as support not only for Angelica but also for that generous lady who contributes so much to this seminary and cares about missions. I was certain she would not be aware of the liberal social views behind Angelica's biblically expressed presentation. And I was equally certain that Angelica would not realize that this was so, that they lived in different cultural worlds. Everyone loved Angelica's talk, which didn't surprise me, for she really had great rapport with the group. From time to time both she and Mrs. Castleton would look over at me for my approval, and to each I would nod back my reassurance. But by pretending to be in agreement with both of them, I feel like I violated the trust of each, and I am ashamed."

Tucker did not like being put in the role of a father confessor, and his first instinct was to tell Batson to lighten up and not take himself so seriously, but he checked himself and said neither when Batson added, "You don't know how unworthy it feels to be deceptive."

They had talked on for awhile and then agreed to tell Angelica to invite any friends she wished to come for pizza and discuss her presentation the next week at Tucker's. When Batson left, after thanking him for lending an ear, Tucker phoned Angelica who expressed her great pleasure at the idea and asked if along with her student friends it would be OK for her also to invite Professor Broadside.

The pizza party the following week, that had grown to about a dozen, had gone well with everyone enjoying themselves and no hint from Batson about his earlier misgivings. After listening with interest to Angelica's report the conversation turned to job prospects for the summer. It was understood that for most students at Star-Cross summer employment was an economic necessity. Asked about her plans, Angelica said that she wasn't sure, but she was looking into possibilities for summer work in Atlanta. "Excellent idea, Angelica," Broadside enthused, clapping her hands for her star pupil. "I'll make contacts to be sure you are directed to the best positions."

Darting an undisclosed glance at Batson, Tucker was certain he detected an instant blush.

Episode 19

Seminary's Non-Discrimination Ethos Leads to Local Gay Rights Conflict

THE ONSET OF SPRING brought heightened pressures for the seminary to increase its number of new student applications as well as its funding for the coming fall. To this end Star-Cross had secured from the Castleton Trust an extra promotional grant to expand its media advertising. In preparation for a new website a high-tech design team had been brought in under President Longshot's instructions to enhance the school's reputation as a different kind of seminary, as its name suggested, where the emphasis was decidedly upon spirituality, rather than theology, in contrast to the parochialism of most American seminaries still bound by the academic traditions of Western Christendom. The difference, as Longshot repeatedly tried to explain in recruiting prospective students, was between a sensibility shaped less by theological metaphors of solidity, suggestive of grounding, such as "foundations," "solid rock," "grounds for faith," and the like, and spiritual metaphors more attuned to fluidity such as "breath," "air," and "wind." To this an overseas visiting scholar, for whom English colloquialisms were not his native tongue, had once responded most favorably by commending the President for "having broken new wind on the subject."

"What we need," Longshot insisted, "is more press and name recognition for the unique place that we are." In further brandishing Star-Cross's *pan-pneumatic* reputation in this manner Longshot confided to Tucker that he realized he was walking a tightrope with the Castleton Trust. But he frankly doubted how much Mildred Castleton would be aware of these days, especially as it came to the Internet, and at any rate he knew he could continue to rely on the good services of Tucker as his liaison to make sure their essential benefactor always retained her favorable impressions.

Proposals from the design team, that met with Longshot's approval, included website images of Star-Cross students variously posed as if in contemplative reflection in the Self-Expression Center and a streaming video of a visually corralled faculty, supplemented with extras to appear twice its size, strolling meditatively throughout the Sacred Garden, and all with an audio background of recorded Tibetan OM mantra chanting suffused throughout.

Tucker had hoped that the new promotional campaign might highlight features of what he considered to be one of Star-Cross's really noteworthy strengths, and that was its declared opposition to bigotry and its allegiance to equal rights. Since its inception the seminary had embodied a policy of human rights and anti-discrimination well before it had become generally popular or institutionally commonplace in comparable schools and seminaries to do so. No doubt, as Tucker often regretted having to admit, it was the very lack at Star-Cross of official ties with any church or religious institutions that had actually enabled this early human rights commitment to full equality.

What had first been expressed without notoriety as a simply stated affirmation of ethnic and sexual equality at its founding a mere twenty years ago had with the changing times come to be explicitly spelled out in ever expanding letters as a commitment from *LGBT*, to *LGBTQ*, to *LGBTQIA*, to *LGBTQIASGL*, to *LGBTQIASGLME* solidarity, as the constantly extending acronym for lesbian, gay, bisexual, transgender, queer, intersex, asexual, same-gender-loving, and marriage equality rights currently expressed it.

To guarantee that the seminary's commitment ever remained unqualifiedly all embracing, in keeping with its *pan-pneumatic* ethos, no matter how many more letters of the alphabet might need to be added in the future, creative Star-Cross students in recent years had designed an original seminary banner inscribed with the words, *Entire Alphabet Rights.* Star-Cross had been among the first in the nation to adopt this human rights insignia that hung understood and unopposed in the Self-Expression Center where its importance was duly emphasized each year to incoming classes at their orientation.

This put the seminary on an uneasy footing with its local environment where entrenched social patterns prevailed with their outspoken assumptions about what was, and what was not, in keeping with Christian teaching. For the most part these two cultural worlds managed to co-exist peacefully by mainly ignoring each other. But tensions did erupt, as at a tense summer job interview in town when a male Star-Cross student with no grades in his records because of *LIQ* exemptions threatened to file charges of sexual harassment when an employer told him that to qualify for a job a closer look at his testimonials would be required. On that occasion a quick intervention by the notified seminary with profound apologies to the irate employer for the student's misunderstanding had barely managed to keep the incident from becoming public. "For the sake of the school you must keep your private matters private," Longshot had sternly admonished the offended student, who then had indignantly reminded Longshot that *he* wasn't the one who had sought to make his private matters public.

But now just on the eve of the launching of Star Cross's newly designed web site and advertising campaign social tensions erupted that threatened the seminary's co-existence with the surrounding community as never before. And this time there was no keeping the news of it under wraps. It was not at all "the more press" and "name recognition" that Longshot had been calling for.

For some time hate groups in the area who were spurred on by extremist preachers on talk radio, and the silence of the mainline churches who felt this was none of their business, had been attacking gay right's signs as *Satan's Signs* and those who carried them as Satan's representatives. This reached a crisis point when a small, beleaguered local group of various ages, with no big city or outside support, attempted its first gay pride march and had its handmade signs ripped down by hostile local authorities before a jeering crowd of accusative onlookers. Star-Cross students, who as a rule remained aloof from local affairs, in hearing reports of this local disturbance quickly assembled in a sizeable number and rushed to the scene where they surrounded the frightened marchers as their bodyguards, and escorted them up the hill to the safety of the seminary campus under the hoisted Star-Cross banner of *Entire Alphabet Rights* where they held a rally together at the Self-Expression Center.

The media coverage with its inflammatory front page photographs and local television and radio breaking news commentary had produced such an avalanche of enraged local criticism of the seminary, for reportedly desecrating what had historically been a revered chapel built to honor the memory of Major Castleton, that Longshot in near panic mode had dispatched Tucker on an urgent mission to make sure that Mildred Castleton herself was kept as much as possible in the dark about these charges of sacrilege and persuaded not to believe, what Longshot called, the utter falsehoods being spread to slander the seminary's good name and its completely spiritual reputation. But the live media news coverage with its photos of the Start-Cross campus rallying in protest under a school banner which all the press now referred to *Satan's Alphabet* could not be dismissed as lies, or covered up as misrepresentation.

Determined this time not to deceive, Tucker immediately elicited Batson Belfry's assistance in hopes of framing the whole incident in terms of the Gospel more familiar to the gentle lady and, most of all, respectful of her sensibilities. Tucker did not know where Batson himself, given his evangelical background, stood on gay rights, but he did know that Batson was serious about the Gospel, and this time he really needed his help.

Episode 20

Longshot Sends Tucker and Batson to Reassure Mildred Castleton

BEFORE TUCKER COULD REACH her, Mildred Castleton had contacted him and invited him and Batson to come as soon as convenient. She was quite aware of the news reports that the Star-Cross chapel had been desecrated by Satanic slogans, and though she had no time for hate radio, had tuned in long enough to hear the vitriol being directed against the seminary and its supporters that was on the air. Employees of the Castleton Trust had also informed her of the hostile tone of some of the messages against the seminary received in their office.

"Please tell me, good gentlemen, what all this distressing news is about," Mildred asked as soon as the three of them had been seated together with a glass of sherry in the smaller reading room just off her library that served as the study and personal office she preferred to meet in for close and serious conversations. Tucker, following Longshot's instructions, began by urging that the irresponsible news reports be recognized as misrepresenting the context of the situation. All that had actually happened, he explained, was simply that some students from Star-Cross had gone to the aid of a small group in town who were peacefully protesting discrimination and who had had the picket signs they were carrying ripped up by a hostile crowd for having letters on them that they charged with being "*Satan's Letters.*"

"What kind of letters?," Mildred asked, leaning forward to make sure she understood.

"Just certain letters of the alphabet used these days by groups in protesting for minority rights," Tucker answered, hoping his evasion would be sufficient.

"Letters having to do specifically with rights regarding sex," Batson added, hesitantly clearing his throat, "like *LGBT* and other letters that some people identify themselves by who feel they are discriminated against."

"It's certainly a different day we live in as far as these movements are concerned," Mildred observed, "and I don't pretend to understand it all."

"Not like the way you and I were raised, is it?," Tucker acknowledged, smiling.

"Not like the way I was brought up, either," Batson commented. "There just seem to be no limits in some people's views today, no restrictions. The banner that some of the Star-Cross students carried in support of the protesters whose letters on their own homemade picket signs were attacked as `Satan's letters' carried the words *Entire Alphabet Rights*. The intention was to be supportive of those protesters who were being jeered as evil, but of course *Entire Alphabet Rights* could also be mistaken to mean that anything goes, and that nothing in the entire alphabet is contrary to Christian teaching. And we know that isn't so."

"And that is why," Tucker continued, "President Longshot has told us to assure you in no uncertain terms that the Star-Cross students who carried the provocative banner saying *Entire Alphabet Rights* that you see photographed in the newspapers will be reprimanded for bringing discredit upon the seminary and most importantly for disrespecting the hallowed memory of the Major's Chapel. He promises that no banner with these words on it, or anything remotely like an entire alphabet reference, will be allowed in the future to desecrate the spiritual sanctity of the chapel honoring the good name of your father for which Star-Cross is so indebted to you and the Castleton Trust. The President further requests that you and the Castleton Trust advise the seminary about your wishes for a new memorial that most fully honors your father's good name to be installed in a reconsecrated chapel that henceforth will be safeguarded from all protest rallies and set aside solely as the center of spiritual devotion it is meant to be. You have his emphatic word, despite whatever slanders you may be hearing, that this is his firm position."

"And is it yours?," Mildred asked, looking at both of them and clearly pondering what she had been assured, weighing their words but giving no indication of what she thought. Surprised by her question, Tucker hesitated for a moment and then punted, "We must do what is most in keeping with the good name of your father as being the best for Star-Cross."

"Papa was a good man," Mrs. Castleton sighed. "I wish you gentlemen could have known him. I agree, we must not desecrate his memory."

As the time came to leave, Batson asked if they could have a word of prayer together. Tucker resisted intrusions of piety in such circumstances and as always was suspicious of its manipulations, but when the dear lady responded, "Oh, yes," he reluctantly joined hands while Batson prayed, briefly expressing thanksgiving for God's grace, and asking that they be guided always in being its faithful witnesses.

After thanking them most cordially as always for coming, and saying she would continue to follow events closely and in due time be back in touch about the President's request for a new memorial honoring her father in reconsecrating the chapel, Mildred Castleton waved good-bye as they headed down the tree shrouded lane and returned to the highway.

On the drive back Tucker and Batson acknowledged by their silence that they were not certain they had made the best case to reassure their concerned host, but, truth be told, neither of them was sure what the other thought the best case was. Both wanted to believe that they had not lied to her regarding the facts, as they suspected Longshot was quite prepared to do, but it was unseemly to try and explain today's sexual equality issues with someone of her background and generation. They agreed that the gracious lady had not exactly found their explanations reassuring, and they also agreed, given her cultural circumstances, that this was to be expected.

Episode 21

Elements of Missing Reliquary Remains Discovered in Sacred Garden

FERDINAND LYZER, THE CHIEF landscape architect and grounds-keeper at Star-Cross, had been at the seminary since its inception, as had Tucker, and through the years the two had become close friends. A favorite on campus of both faculty and students alike, where he was popularly known by the name he had always gone by of *Ferdie*, Lyzer was chiefly responsible for maintaining the Sacred Garden surrounding the Self-Expression Center which had been reconstructed from what had originally been designated as the Major's Chapel in memory of Mildred Castleton's father. Now in the wake of the gay pride disturbances that had turned local opinion sharply against the seminary the Center was soon to be reconsecrated. Hopefully, from the administration's point of view, this would gain back some support of the locals who revered the historical Castleton legacy.

As part of this reconsecration effort Lyzer had been put in charge of expanding the Sacred Garden and enhancing its attraction as an inviting place of pilgrimage and spiritual retreat. He was eminently qualified for this assignment by having trained as a botanist specializing in botanical gardening before later becoming recognized as one of the best landscape design architects in the area. But equally important was the fact that the Lyzers were Catholics for whom a sense of the sacred was a vocation. Ferdie and his wife and their four children were regulars at mass in the town's parish church, where he also served as the caretaker of the adjoining graveyard and painstakingly preserved its oldest, moss covered tombstones, several of which bore the still discernible mark of the ancient Latin blessing *R I P* ("Rest in Peace"). Tucker had been honored to be invited to attend the first communion mass of each of the four Lyzer children who had grown up considering *Uncle Tuck* a member of the family.

In their on campus association through the years the two friends had found themselves, more often than not, sharing the same, often bemused, but always loyal, reaction to seminary events. With the raise of an eyebrow each could communicate with the other when suddenly called into service by one of President Longshot's impromptu directives without having to utter a word. Such had been the case when together they had hurriedly militarized the Buddha statue with a Halloween helmet and rifle to make Mildred Castleton, peering from her car at a distance, think it was a statue of her father, the old Major. And together they had just as quickly ducked from view at the sudden arrival on the scene of a distraught Professor Broadside and her visiting bus load of shocked peace seekers to prevent them from knowing who had been the culprit disfiguring the Compassionate Buddha and humiliating them in this manner. Together they had managed to position the heavy bronze marker donated by the dear lady to mark the "Way to the Sacred Garden" so that the words "of Gethsemane" that she had without notice added were hidden by the surrounding foliage from public view. But most of all they had both experienced the debacle of Wisteria Dean's interim administration during a Longshot sabbatical when her ill-conceived attempt to promote *Criss-Cross Tours* of the Sacred Garden as a money raising endeavor had led to the discovery of the loss of the reliquary of St. Fabula raising suspicions about the misappropriation of its intended endowment funds as bequeathed to the seminary by the excommunicated local order of *The Amazon Sisters of St. Fabula.* Like most Catholics in town Ferdie had viewed the sisters as unorthodox, joking to Tucker that he never saw them at mass. "People used to say that they made up their own mass for themselves, and didn't need a priest to hear their confessions. They definitely weren't traditional, that's for sure. But they were always interesting to me in their freedom to be themselves, regardless of criticism, and they were very generous in wanting to pay me whenever I did any work for them on the grounds of their convent—which of course I wouldn't accept. I guess the only pope they chose to obey was our Pope Joan," he added, as they both nodded, grinning. "But I had nothing against them, and I feel bad that the relics they entrusted to us are rumored to have somehow gotten mixed up in the load of small rocks ordered for the construction of our campus garden. That sure didn't bring any credit to us as a seminary."

"Longshot really swept that one under the rug," Tucker remarked.

"Or under the dirt," Ferdie added. "But now with this chance for another try we have got to figure out how best to turn the situation around and restore this peaceful setting to what it was meant to be."

Tucker had agreed, and among the plans they researched and discussed was the installation of a new labyrinth, or walking maze, for meditation on the grounds of the Sacred Garden patterned after the famous twelfth century exemplar in the historic pathway floor of *Chartres Cathedral,* but with ancient antecedents in many cultures dating back over three thousand years to prehistoric times. Longshot had been pleased by this idea so long as the design incorporated a *pan-pneumatic* range of sources.

It was in the spade work for this new labyrinth that a discovery was made by one of Lyzer's crew that later brought the two together again in the President's office with news that none of the three had dreamed likely.

A text message from Ferdie alerted Tucker that an apparent shard had surfaced in excavations at the Sacred Garden that at least merited examination as a possible clue to the whereabouts of St. Fabula's missing reliquary. A weathered porcelain fragment of less than two inches across its jagged broken edge had turned up in the digging that revealed the barely detectable marking *R I P.* On the reverse side in a tiny inscription decipherable only with a strong magnifying glass one Latin variant of the ancient blessing of "rest in peace" appeared faintly visible, *Requiem in pacem.* At least, the letters *Requiem in pa . . . m* could be guessed at, with a worn blank between the *pa* and the *m* in *pacem.* Since a single tooth had also been found in some pebbles nearby, and a thumbnail sized sand patch that to the untrained eye could be imagined and touted as powdered bone, it was agreed that the President should be made aware at once.

Not surprisingly, to either Ferdie or Tucker, Longshot reacted with such instant enthusiasm at these findings and the thought of how they could currently advantage the seminary in its attempt to regain some profitable publicity that he insisted no expert authentication of the remnants would be necessary. Nor would any proof be needed that "the scraps" as he called them even belonged together. All that mattered was that the media design team immediately create an inspiring closed replica encasement for veneration by devout visitors with the filled in letters of the Latin blessing inscribed over the name *St. Fabula of Amazonia* and installed next to the window of Pope Joan. While this new display installation would be set up independently of the reconsecration service being planned for the Self-Expression Center and the honoring of the memory of Major Castleton, it would, Longshot declared with great satisfaction, add to the spiritual pluralism of the coinciding occasion to have it in place.

The pluralism Longshot insisted upon proved to be a more complex network of sensibilities to coordinate in planning the reconsecration of the Self-Expression Center than anyone had initially foreseen. The occasion demanded that four considerations be taken into account. First of all, and most crucial in Tucker's mind, was that no minimizing be done to Star-Cross's long-standing policy of non-discrimination and equal human rights, including *LGBT* rights, which could be interpreted by the public as a seminary course correction. This possibility he found especially worrisome in light of the administration's repeated disclaimer after the recent disturbances of all banner references to *Entire Alphabet Rights*. There was secondly, and most obviously, the consideration that the historic dependence of the seminary on the beneficence of the Castleton Trust required that the heritage of Reformed Christianity with its biblical emphasis also not be simply discarded, even if only by avoidance out of hand. There was third the question of how to weave these elements together in a reconsecration of the Self-Expression Center with the enlarged Sacred Garden that paid tribute to the memory of Major Castleton. And fourth was the need to incorporate the spiritual significance of the reconstructed reliquary of St. Fabula into the favorable publicity that the newly designed seminary website would give to the entire event.

Wisely, in Tucker's view, the administration had placed primary responsibility for dealing with these considerations into the hands of interested students willing to engage in the planning. Several faculty advisers had been selected by the students themselves to help out, and Tucker was relieved to see the names of Professors Broadside and Belfry among them. This meant, he had rightly suspected, that Angelica Blankchek had agreed to take a leadership role in the planning, and he could not think, given the particular circumstances, of a better positioned coordinator.

Since the media design team was most anxious to get the new reliquary discovery up and running on the seminary website as soon as possible priority was given to expedite this project that lamentably resulted in its initial undoing, at least for the time being. After hastily installing the enclosed casement with the restored lettering on the wall just above it a small seminary group had been assembled to be filmed lighting candles around it. This group which designated itself the *Devotees of Joan the 116th* , as the disputed ninth century successor to Peter was numbered in succession among the Roman pontiffs, met regularly for meditation at the Pope Joan window to show their solidarity, as they expressed it, with all "the unacknowledged and the disregarded." In this instance their announced aim was to give public notice of the restored reliquary of the disregarded St. Fabula by chanting in the glow of candlelight the words of the Latin blessing rest in peace so that the necessary filming could be completed and put on line.

Almost immediately irreverent reaction to the website had been forthcoming, and within less than twenty-four hours the lampooning on social media had become so devastating that the video was abruptly taken down. The uncertain Latin presumed to be *Requiem in pacem* had been mistakenly transcribed on the wall above the reliquary as *Requiem in partem* eliciting a slew of ridiculing responses that the botched rest in peace blessing of St. Fabula more aptly read *Rest in Pieces.*

Episode 22

The Reconsecration of the Chapel to Commemorate Major Castleton

THE OTHER CONSIDERATIONS REGARDING plans for the reconsecration of the Self-Expression Center proved to be more successfully navigated. Batson kept Tucker informed, and Tucker was encouraged to see Batson's influence on the arrangements. In effect the program would be an enactment of the import of Angelica's research thesis on *The Spiritual Significance of Anti-Normativity in Ancient Hindu Eroticism* but tailored to conform to the biblical idiom along the lines in which she had recast it with Batson's advisement for her presentation to the great approval of Mildred Castleton's Bible Fellowship Group. Tucker reflected on the difficulty he had experienced in finding a necessarily biblical sounding theme for the program of the earlier cornerstone laying of the Center that was not deemed too exclusively Christian for the faculty to accept. In that case the only agreement finally achievable had been on *The Wind Bloweth Where It Will*. But now with the controversy over sexual rights and the additional element of physicality it introduced adding to the complexity, the planning committee had managed the nearly impossible by selecting for the reconsecration theme *Gird Up Your Loins*.

This had not come about without having to deal with objections. Rigore Mortisse had apparently spoken for several in admonishing that the unseemly mention of loins served to exacerbate the very problem that the spiritual reconsecration was meant to address. Isadora Broadside upon first hearing had instantly opposed the theme as sexist but had reconsidered after further good natured conversation with Angelica. In fact, as Tucker gathered from Batson, Angelica's leadership had been quite impressive. Arguing that modesty does not mean denial, and that it was truer to the message of the Bible to see the body as a good creation, and a temple of the spirit, she had to Batson's amazement countered Mortisse by even drawing upon the words of the Apostle Paul to the Corinthians that "God has so composed the body, giving the greater honor to the inferior part" (*1 Cor.* 12:24). Acknowledging that Job is indeed twice told out of the whirlwind to "gird up your loins like a man" (*Job* 38:3, 40:7), she had teasingly reminded Professor Broadside that in *Proverbs* it is the virtuous woman who is praised by saying, "She girds her loins with strength" (*Prov.* 31:17). "Yes, but that's only because she's credited as a wife," Broadside had retorted laughing, "but I'll grant your point."

Angelica had clearly done her homework, and she did not neglect to take into account the legitimate concern that Star-Cross's *Entire Alphabet Rights* banner could be misinterpreted as sanctioning moral indifference, something Batson had pointed out to Mrs. Castleton when he and Tucker had their urgent meeting with her in her home. The biblical appeal to "gird up," Angelica had stressed to the planning committee, would serve to underscore that "equal rights" does not mean that anything goes. There is no right to do harm or to abuse.

By the time the day set for the reconsecration had arrived the results of the weeks of planning were evident in the handsomely printed program notes distributed to all in attendance. A medley of diverse elements had so artfully been brought together under the theme of *Gird Up Your Loins* that it was as if a jigsaw puzzle when completed had provided the picture of a reconsecration at once arguably biblical yet accommodating to Star-Cross's non-exclusivist pluralism. The service began with a welcome and statement of purpose by the President that included special recognition of Mildred Castleton and the friends accompanying her from her church as well as the Castleton Trust. Angelica Blankchek, as the planning chair, then introduced the program's theme by first briefly highlighting its biblical context and then stepping aside for the enactment of its multi-dimensional spiritual significance by a variety of participants. First, from one side of the room male voices began faintly chanting in almost OM-like mantra repetition the scriptural text from *Job* (33:3, 40:7), "out of the whirlwind, gird up your loins like a man," while from the opposite side equally faint female voices took up the chant in a slightly higher register with words from *Proverbs* (31:17), "she girds her loins with strength." As the volume of the alternating chants gradually increased a group of students in liturgical tunics began a stately dance in circuitous simulation of the Last Supper and the washing of feet while the chanters slowly moved toward each other from their opposing sides to join hands encircling the entire room while intermingling their raised voices in an atonal harmony by singing together the words of Jesus from the *Gospel of Luke* (12:35), "Let your loins be girded and your lamps burning."

The ritual performance suggestive of foot washing then continued with the entrance of another group led by the lamps burning *Devotees of Joan the 116th* also chanting antiphonally, but now, so the program noted, in a modified form of Gregorian tradition. The audience was invited to join in singing a number of rounds of the antiphon in its ancient Latin text *Ubi caritas et amor, Deus ibi est*, translated in the program notes as, "Where charity and love are, God is there."

After an interlude of Professor Broadside and her sacred lute music which she had listed in the program, rather disparagingly of others, Tucker thought, as a "respite" (rather than interlude) for meditation following what had gone before, the vested Gospel Choir from the historically black Baptist Church in town entered singing in step with the rhythm of the spiritual, *Every Time I Feel The Spirit*. Emmaus Baptist was the only church in the area that had spoken out publicly in support of the marchers and Star-Cross students when attacked and an appreciative seminary suddenly feeling very much alive in the Spirit joined in the clapping, Mildred being, Tucker noticed, among them. Their second rendition, *There's a Sweet, Sweet Spirit in This Place,* with the words, "*and I know it is the Spirit of the Lord*" transitioned into a procession incorporating participants from a variety of sacred traditions, including Native Americans and two Muslim friends of Angelica's from college days. An Aaronic Blessing was then powerfully chanted in Hebrew as a benediction over the entire assembly by the Cantor from a local synagogue, with many responding to the words, "*The Lord lift up his countenance upon you, and give you peace,*" with a fervent AMEN.

With this order of ritual now concluded, and quite successfully Tucker thought, the program was turned over to the representatives of the Castleton Trust for the unveiling of the Major Castleton memorial. Tucker had not been unaware of some behind the hands snickering and whispers during the proceedings from a few of his more disgruntled colleagues that a dispirited Star-Cross from now on would apparently be forced to pay its bills by becoming a producer of amateur Sunday School pageants. The memorial itself had not been disclosed by the Castleton Trust, even to Longshot or the program committee, but the general expectation was that it would be either a prestigious plaque most likely of marble or such, or quite possibly a newly commissioned formal portrait painted from one of the Major's old black and white photographs in uniform. Neither option evoked much enthusiasm on a campus still demoralized by Longshot's removal and prohibition of the *Entire Alphabet Rights* banner from the Self-Expression Center. But there was an undisputed acquiescence in the seminary community that at this critical juncture a show of respect was essential if Star-Cross was to exist.

As the audience was invited to gather round, an executive from the Castleton Trust read a biographical sketch of the Major and spoke of the role of the Castleton family in the history of the seminary. Mildred Castleton herself was then ushered up to pull

85

the cord unveiling the mounted bequest. As the covering fell to the floor an exclamation arose from the entire center. Amazingly, a towering banner was raised to the rafters that clearly no one—unless perhaps Angelica, Tucker wondered—could possibly have imagined. On a rich tapestry of the bold rainbow colors of the gay rights flag the words in brilliant gold letters had been sown, *The Spirit of Love from A to Z.* While recording cameras rolled and mobile devices clicked a cheer resounded as the whole room burst into applause. Being entreated to please speak a word, the dear lady referred to the bequest as her gift to the students in remembrance of the rainbow sign of the everlasting covenant made with Noah and every living creature for all future generations (*Gen.* 9:13). "My personal gratitude must be expressed to the seminary design team," she said, "for first suggesting this colorful background and securing the fabric for us in our church Bible Fellowship to sew on the gold letters. And the men in our group especially wanted me to let you know that even a few of them took a turn in adding their stitches."

Then turning to Tucker she reached for his hand and clutching it before the cameras added, "Since, as I remember Professor Schmoot pointing out to me, Star-Cross already has a monument to the likeness of Major Castleton's stature in the Sacred Garden, I wanted this chapel memorial to be a likeness of his heart."

Episode 23

Longshot Senses Threat to His Authority in the Reconsecration Service

MOST EVERYONE HAD LEFT the reconsecration ceremony with an intense feeling of relief if not elation. Respect had been paid and values maintained. Tucker conveyed his appreciation to Angelica and the planning committee for their successful efforts and congratulated all who had taken part. Star-Cross had weathered the public attacks heaped upon it, and with the uncanny support of its resolute patron and the Castleton Trust had been brought to the truest articulation for which it had been searching of what it stood for, *The Spirit of Love from A to Z*. The reconsecration ceremony had set the tone for guiding the seminary into the immediate future. A biblically sounding rationale would frame Star-Cross's policy and program though the content would consist of a non-exclusive spirituality explicitly distinguished from any religious particularity. While definitions would remain imprecise as with all liquidity metaphors of the spirit, Brother John's characterization of "spiritual" in his outside consultant's lecture on *Fingering Our*

Spiritual Pulse as "anything ultimately intangible connected to the soul" would do for now.

Only Batson had sensed Tucker's tempered enthusiasm upon leaving and was intrigued, given how favorably matters had seemingly turned out, as to why this was the case. "We don't always have to go around with a set smile on our face pretending to feel ecstatic," Tucker had remarked irritably, aware that his comment would score a point precisely where evangelicals were considered most vulnerable. Without missing a beat Batson responded, but not in kind. "That's true, but when I came to you feeling low after Angelica's talk at Mrs. Castleton's I shared the reason. I knew I had been deceptive in betraying someone's trust, people I cared about, and I hurt." Saying no more the matter ended as it was clear that Tucker did not wish to pursue it further. After exchanging a few awkward pleasantries they parted, each going his separate way. Tucker's way, though he had refused to divulge it to his bewildered colleague, was headed straight toward the President's unhappy office, where joined by Lyzer the three of them behind closed doors tried to contemplate the stunning enormity of possible problems resulting from Mildred Castleton's most unanticipated presentation. Longshot was under no misapprehension that the particular choice of the memorial to Major Castleton, whether unintentional on her part as was likely, constituted a direct challenge to his authority by blatantly defying his well publicized prohibition of any future banners at Star-Cross suggestive of *Entire Alphabet Rights.* His leadership of the seminary had been effectively sidelined by the memorial that would now make him a laughing stock of all the students and their supporters whom he had earlier reprimanded. Convinced that he had been outsmarted by his own website design team, whom he suspected without proof of being in collusion with some of the staff of the Castleton Trust, he paced the floor fuming at the marginalized status this new banner threatened to impose upon his position as President.

The final blow, of course, which had left the three of them dumbfounded, with Tucker in full view the most abashedly red faced, had been their benefactor's grateful but innocently erroneous announcement on camera that there was already a Star-Cross memorial monument with Major Castleton's likeness on campus in the Sacred Garden.

"What the hell am I supposed to do now," Longshot fisted his palm, "have another fake Halloween military helmet put back on the head of the Buddha? Oh, that would be nice, now wouldn't it? No problems at all. Why, it could become the logo of our new website, Star-Cross Seminary's own Smokey the Bear."

"I couldn't believe it when Mrs. Castleton made that announcement," Tucker said, shaking his head. "And all the while holding on to my hand for support. Talk about feeling like a complete hypocrite!"

"I'm telling you somebody put her up to it," Longshot continued, "believe me, Castleton herself wouldn't know gay pride from a hay ride." Then checking himself, "Sorry, but I just don't like to see the good woman duped and taken advantage of by others for their own purposes."

Tucker gulped, as Ferdie turned his face away.

"Mortisse immediately confronted me on the way out," Longshot grumbled. "He has his knickers in a twist because he says I allowed, catch that, I *allowed* a gay rights flag raised in the chapel. What's with that stiff? If you ask me he needs to have *his* testimonials checked, if he has any."

"Come on," Ferdie spoke up, not having wanted to seem unserious about his friends' obvious discomfort, "you Protestants need to have a Father Confessor."

"I'm not a Protestant, I'm a very high church Episcopalian," Tucker objected, "at least on occasion, even if you couldn't guess."

"Well I'm surely no WASP," Longshot added. "But you're right, Ferdie, we've got to dispense with this negativity and contemplate our next steps. We three are the only ones who can resolve this, and we want to keep it that way. I'll see to it that the dear lady's innocent comment is cut from the recording, hopefully before anyone questions it, and does not get put on our website."

"As a Catholic who grew up going to confession I'm good for ideas about restitution," Ferdie announced with mock solemnity, "and I have one. I have been going over in my mind Mrs. Castleton's exact words since I wrote them down immediately after she spoke. She said, and I quote, `Star-Cross already has a monument to the likeness of Major Castleton's stature in the Sacred Garden,` and I know how we can make that statement of hers true—maybe not `already,` as she said—but now, and in the future. There will be no lie."

"God, I like your confessional," Tucker said, "but how is this possible? We Episcopalians when we're really high tend to be very pragmatic you know!"

Episode 24

Requested Help from Trustees Puts Castleton Chauffeur in Jeopardy

FERDINAND LYZER'S IDEA, WHICH had alleviated Longshot's and Tucker's distress as soon as they heard it, in retrospect seemed rather simple, but no less brilliant. With the new labyrinth currently being constructed in the expanded Sacred Garden a stone marker to adjoin it had been included in the original design from the beginning. It would now only be a matter of selecting the most advantageous words, in light of the changed circumstances, to be engraved upon it. The three of them agreed to give thought to this proposal and after conferring several times settled upon the following. Across the top of the monument in appropriate calligraphy the name would appear.

THE GIRD UP YOUR LOINS IN LOVE LABYRINTH

This title would provide an instant recall of the labyrinth's connection with the favorably viewed reconsecration ceremony of the Self-Expression Center, and the precisely chosen words underneath would enshrine that connection explicitly for all future visitors.

> *A Monument To The Spiritual Stature Of Major Thomas*
> *Castleton*

This monument wording, as Lyzer had advocated, would align closely enough with Mrs. Castleton's own statement at the reconsecration service to assure that her announcement had been true, or at the very least, to provide for deniability that what she had said was false. Longshot himself had then added a third line of wording at the base of the monument to reaffirm—as he explained it—a non-exclusive pluralistic spiritual link with the soon to be online re-posting of the *St. Fabula* reliquary.

> *And A Requiem in Steps*

This time the *Requiem* blessing would be retranslated with "a postmodern destabilization of meaning" (a favorite term of Longshot's) to read "in steps," rather than "in pieces," thus bringing it more into accord with the pedestrian spirituality of a walking maze and also no longer susceptible to social media's irreverent ridicule.

It was Tucker who then brought up the question of where the money to pay for the engraved monument marker would come from. Struggling to maintain his last shred of conscience in the matter he was adamant that the amount should not be taken from the funds of the new media development grant awarded by the Castleton Trust. "Mrs. Castleton must not be made to bear the cost of her own deception," he insisted.

Longshot said that he totally agreed and reported that as soon as the three of them had decided on the labyrinth marker he had tried to contact the Chair of the Star-Cross Board of Trustees soliciting support but was informed by Daphne Doolittle's executive office that their CEO was out of the country. "On another one of her trips to the Amazon," Longshot scoffed, "collecting more exotic roots and nuts from the rainforest for the business." The office had assured him that she was due back shortly and would be in contact immediately upon her return. "Should have asked her to dig up a few anti-aging specimens in the jungle to bring back as relics for our St. Fabula's reliquary," Longshot commented impatiently. "It's about time she and our Board exerted themselves to do something."

In truth, Longshot had heretofore been quite satisfied having a passive Board to deal with that could be counted on to go along without initiative or objection to whatever he proposed. Since the Castleton Trust had been taken for granted as the insurer of the seminary's financial security, no burden of responsibility had fallen upon the Star-Cross trustees who as a consequence relaxed in their social role as a corporate board of directors not called upon to give direction. As the Board's current Chair selection, Doolittle had struck some observers as the perfect name for its presiding officer.

The trustees were a well intentioned and congenial group of modest philanthropists not bound by doctrinaire religious traditions but willing to lend their names and status to promote causes popularly identified as "spiritual but not religious." They were basically representative of successful secularists, not subject to cultic enticements, but interested in the health benefits of spirituality. They were united, both the women and the men, in their fitness concerns, with a couple superannuated athletic coaches in their number and several younger members as likely to show up at the semiannual dinner meetings in their golfing or jogging attire as in tailored business suits. These twice a year board dinner meetings customarily commenced as the culmination of an over extended happy hour, which Longshot in his abstinence managed mostly to skip. They were routinely conducted without agenda but always opened with a moment that some members considered prayer and others meditation, but that all agreed should be kept brief and speechless. As the designated Honorary Chair since Star-Cross's founding, Mildred Castleton herself seldom attended but always saw to it that a representative was present from the Castleton Trust.

This meant that in soliciting the Board for some further contributions Longshot would not be able to reveal exactly what they were needed for. No mention obviously could be made about the newly devised labyrinth marker required to verify Mildred Castleton's innocent but erroneous claim that Star-Cross had a monument to the likeness of her father's stature in its Sacred

Garden. Instead, in his conversation with Doolittle he had simply emphasized that the additional funds were necessary to provide enhancements to the Sacred Garden. Given the Chairwoman's online marketing firm that she and her retired husband owned and that she now operated, Longshot knew that appeals for "enhancements" were most likely to win her approval. Overjoy Enhancement Marketing Inc. featured a menu of natural products sold under four main classifications advertized as garden, nutritional, cosmetic, and emotional enhancements. "Notions, potions, and lotions for emotions," is how Longshot referred to them in the confidence of Tucker and Ferdie.

The firm in the past had generously provided items from its nutritional menu for the teas Longshot hosted in his presidential office during Mildred Castleton's annual visits, and he reminded Doolittle how much her firm's *Overjoy Biscuits* especially had been favored by the dear lady. "Oh do let us mail you several cartons to give Mrs. Castleton as a surprise token of the Board's affection," Daphne responded enthusiastically, indicating no recollection of how samples of Overjoy's *Wrinkles Away* enhancement lotion had once mistakenly gotten included in the packaging. As they continued their conversation about possible ways for the Board to make further contributions a deal was reached that an online link to Overjoy products would be made available on the Star-Cross website. For a trial period Overjoy Marketing would donate a percentage of each online sale to Star-Cross, and without candidly saying so it was tacitly understood that the respectability gained by being associated with spirituality via the seminary could benefit Overjoy in turn by potentially making the company less vulnerable to the suspicions of possible illegalities that food and drug agents constantly raise toward those in the merchandizing of innovative natural products. Longshot was aware that such a commercial online link between Star-Cross's and Overjoy's websites would not please the seminary's new media design team. Nor in fact were Tucker and Ferdie pleased when he told them. But, as he explained to the two, by rallying the Board to his side the arrangement remedied the financial problem of the moment and would also serve to remind any who might wish to circumvent his leadership of who was still in charge. It did appear at least that a serious dilemma had been averted, and as Ferdie resumed his supervision of the Sacred Garden's expansion Tucker returned to his teaching with his mind now free to concentrate upon his courses.

When the biscuit gift cartons for Mrs. Castleton arrived from Overjoy in Longshot's office he notified the staff of the Castleton Trust of the Board's present for their Honorary Chair and was advised that Clarence would be driving into town the following morning to have his chauffeur's license renewed and the Chrysler given a safety inspection and would pick up the cartons earlier at the seminary on his way in. It was much later that afternoon when Tucker received a most urgent distress call from one of the Trust attorneys asking that he please meet him as soon as possible at the Division of Motor Vehicles inspection station concerning a critical matter regarding the Castleton chauffeur. Going immediately he found a visibly shaken Clarence being detained for questioning by police investigators on suspicion of violating interstate commerce law by transporting out of state sales of cannabis cookies. Both the renewal of his chauffeur's license and the keys to the Chrysler had been withheld along with the confiscated cartons from Overjoy intended as a surprise tribute to the dear lady that had been discovered in the trunk. For over an hour while the Castleton attorney conferred with the officers to settle the matter and secure a release, Tucker, after providing a character witness, sat with Clarence who with his cap tightly clutched in one hand continued to rub his forehead with the other in anxiety over the upset this incident would surely cause his matron, quietly repeating as if to himself, "Never so much as had a traffic ticket in all my years of driving."

Episode 25

Longshot Seeks Quick Funds by Arranging an Unlikely Prayer Breakfast

Tucker never learned the full details of the negotiations that had fortunately resulted in Clarence's release without a formal filing of charges or any notation made on his renewed chauffeur's license. As a personal gift to boost his distressed friend he had persuaded Clarence to let him pay for a new cap. He did learn subsequently from Longshot that investigators had also come to his office questioning his role as the recipient of the out of state cartons picked up by Clarence for delivery and to Overjoy Marketing's corporate headquarters itself as the producer. Ironically, this was the very sort of investigation that Overjoy's proposed link with the Star-Cross website had been envisioned to ward off, but now the deal that had so recently been agreed to had effectively cancelled itself even before becoming operative. This left Longshot with the imperative to come up quickly with some alternative idea to help attract the immediate capital required to underwrite the reconfigured labyrinth monument.

Doolittle, eager to repair any damage to either of them, in a hastily faxed message explaining she would be away on a business trip with her research staff exploring the enhancement benefits of glacial fungi in Greenland, had provided Longshot with a further suggestion about a possible source of quick revenue that he found both repellent and yet impelled by financial necessity to follow up. It was this suggestion which would bring Tucker and Batson back together as Longshot's designees to carry out. The Chairwoman had also offered as compensation to substitute a full array of Overjoy's gastric and cosmetic enhancements as the appreciation gift from the Board for Mildred Castleton, but Longshot, wincing at this potion and lotion notion, responded that it might be best to wait until a more opportune time to see what product innovations the glacial fungi exploration uncovered.

Doolittle's fax informed Longshot about an association of Christian corporate executives who held prayer breakfasts periodically at schools throughout the nation in furtherance of their aims. The group traced its historic origins back to the opposition in the nineteen thirties to Franklin Roosevelt's New Deal policies that were attacked by major leaders of industry as Socialistic and had initially gone by the name *Capitalists for Christ.* That name was later changed to *Business By The Bible Prayer Associates* who had then adopted as the group's byline logo on all its publications and promotional literature, "*His Business is Our Business.*" In the tradition of the wealthy corporate moguls known for reportedly having mailed free copies of conservative Protestant tracts famously called *The Fundamentals* to all seminaries, pastors, and Sunday Schools throughout the English speaking world during 1910–1915, this current *Business By The Bible* off-shoot of executives contributed generously to those colleges and seminaries which they deemed to foster within their students a fundamental Christianity consistent with an unregulated market economy. To this end they held their prayer breakfasts in schools recommended as deserving of their support where they offered five hundred dollar awards to any two students chosen by the host school as representative of its biblical teaching who agreed to prepare a personal "testimony" for delivery at their breakfasts based upon a Gospel passage chosen for them by the association with instructions to testify to what that text says to us about doing "business by the Bible."

At the conclusion of each of the meetings an offering of checks and pledges of contributions was then collected for the support of the host school. Doolittle assured Longshot that, depending upon the number of members present and how favorable an impression the school made, donations when totaled not infrequently amounted to a lucrative gift of some twenty to thirty thousand dollars. Writing an individual check contribution for much less than a thousand dollars, she quipped, was viewed by this association as a personal embarrassment.

Daphne frankly admitted to Longshot that she and her husband seldom bothered to attend the breakfasts, but maintained their active membership and donations solely for the business contacts affording them commercial advantage. Despite the title of prayer breakfasts, she confessed that she personally found the meetings to consist less of prayer and more of politics couched in the rhetoric of a bible-quoting piety. "Not exactly," she added, "my spiritual cup of tea."

Notwithstanding this cautionary criticism, when Daphne insisted that her husband's recommendation and influence could definitely see to it that one of the forthcoming executive prayer breakfasts was scheduled at Star-Cross *if* the President so wished, Longshot immediately jumped to the offer, emphasizing to Tucker and Ferdie that he was only willing to set aside Star-Cross's *panpneumatic* pluralism and overlook the exclusivist Protestant fundamentalism of the prayer group's capitalism "for Christ" so long as this one time "strategic venture," as he described it, resulted in quick capital for Star-Cross.

"It's called 'venture capitalism,'" Ferdie had whispered out of the side of his mouth to Tucker, keeping a straight face as Longshot, not noticing, continued.

"Just a 'strategic' rendering unto Caesar," Tucker had responded under his breath.

To imagine a fund raising project more contrary to Star-Cross's self-proclaimed *pan-pneumatic* commitments would be hard indeed, but Longshot defending the proposal against Tucker's and Ferdie's skepticism had insisted that no one need imagine it. The three of them would keep this matter to themselves. Only "the young evangelical," as Longshot referred to Batson, would additionally have to be involved as someone essential to the undertaking, and Longshot reiterated his reliance upon Tucker to make sure that Batson performed his necessary role while remaining innocent of the scheme of things propelling their efforts.

Looking back it would be easy to see why Longshot's preconception of Batson had led the President to bank upon Star-Cross's most junior faculty member as his ace card in guaranteeing that he played a winning hand in such an implausible situation.

Episode 26

Batson Is Recruited to Make Star-Cross Appear Evangelical

IT WAS SOME MONTHS before an agreeable Saturday date for the prayer breakfast meeting could be negotiated. With the academic year just ending and summer school sessions yet to begin the weekend campus would be mostly deserted with its facilities closed, making it an ideal time for any influx of unlikely visitors to come and go unnoticed. The dining hall would be reserved for a catered brunch buffet, arranged and financed by the seminary, and set to begin with the association's customary opening hymn sing and table grace at mid-morning followed by a program that included remarks by the President, with the "testimonies" of the two selected students in the later afternoon, concluding with the collection of gift checks and pledges of donations that would be totaled and mailed back to the seminary.

Longshot had spoken with Batson about how his assistance and participation could serve the seminary as only he, of all the faculty, with his evangelical background could. It was the first time the President had ever made any acknowledgement of his background or his teaching, and Batson expressed his eagerness to do whatever he could for the good of the seminary. He was especially happy to be teamed up with his trusted mentor whom Longshot told him would supply the necessary details as they planned together for the coming occasion.

"There's really only one main thing I want you to do," Longshot said, "just one—besides of course joining in the activities and praying the breakfast blessing when I introduce you—and that is see to it that the two Star-Cross students Tucker and you choose to speak to this group deliver a really evangelical sounding 'testimony', as this group calls it, that will convince potential donors in attendance that Star-Cross's biblical teaching is fundamentally true Gospel teaching and deserving of their financial support."

Tucker and Batson had given careful consideration to selecting the two best representative students they believed most able and willing to prepare their own testimony on the texts assigned to them: in the one case *Luke* 2:29, "Know you not that I must be about my Father's business?," and in the other, *Luke* 19:23, "Why did you not put my money in the bank and collect interest?" These students, a woman and a man both with serious commitments to their biblical studies, could also well use the five hundred dollar awards as they faced their financial needs for the summer.

For his part Tucker had consented to assist Longshot in preparing some suitable presidential remarks for such an improbable setting that, as Longshot himself acknowledged, put him at risk for being scented as the proverbial skunk at a church picnic. Assembling some lines from his typical recruitment addresses on the benefits of spirituality, Tucker's general guidance to Longshot was that he stick to his familiar scripts but change his references from "spirituality" to the "Spirit of Jesus Christ." Batson's guidance to the two students he was asked to prepare basically reviewed with them the points of exegesis that they studied in class, which first and foremost involved listening to the text before interpreting it, and doing so in its four contexts, that of its origin and its original language if possible, that of how it sounds in relation to other texts within the scriptural canon of which it is part, that of noting the history of its hearing as expressed in commentaries, and that of how it is heard in the present day context of its listeners. Both

Tucker and Batson were resolute that they would not attempt to put words in the students' mouths, which, as Batson observed to Tucker's concurrence would contradict the meaning of a personal testimony since they were not God. They would wait with expectancy to hear what the students had to say when they spoke and not ask to read over their prepared remarks for possible changes or corrections ahead of time.

Longshot himself had further asked Tucker to supply some sentences for him to read in calling Batson up front to the microphone as representative of the seminary to deliver the breakfast blessing as soon as the meeting convened. Embarrassed at hearing himself introduced in such overblown and out of character remarks by the President as, "Star-Cross's evangelical servant of the only-begotten saving Word made flesh, crucified and risen, ascended and coming, who bears such faithful witness to the Gospel in all his teaching, so that, as on the Day of Pentecost, by the power of the Holy Spirit all are enabled to hear and understand wherever they are coming from as if in their own native tongue," Batson, suspecting the ghost writer's hand, looked quizzically at Tucker, who from the other side of the room winked back at him knowingly. After joining in a rousing chorus of *I Love to Tell The Story,* which Batson knew by heart but took pains in his singing not to startle the uncomprehending President who was faking the words next to him, or embarrass his High Church Episcopalian mentor with any undue fervor, the momentarily anointed Star-Cross junior professor offered without pretense the opening prayer of grateful hearts for all the blessings of this life that had brought them to this hour and for the food they were now about to partake of in table fellowship together ever mindful of the needs of others in Jesus' name.

Episode 27

The Prayer Breakfast Is Held

WHEN THE MEAL HAD concluded the presiding officer called upon Batson to stand up again and lead the assembly in the singing of *Stand Up, Stand Up For Jesus*. This was followed in the day's program by several of the association's members, apparently as was the routine, offering in turn their economic commentary on the overtaxed prospects of the market that in each instance concluded with a call to, "Let us pray," urging accelerated economic expansion with less government regulation.

This jarringly cryptic ritual, in Tucker's view, nevertheless provided an ideal segue for Longshot's ensuing presidential remarks which began with a well received emphatic assertion that "the Spirit of Jesus Christ is *not* subject to regulation." Tucker breathed a sigh of relief as heads began to nod in instant agreement, with even a few robust "Amens" uttered around the room. Longshot had established his orthodoxy. Even his less successful substituting of the words "Spirit of Jesus Christ" in place of his usual references to "spirituality," as Tucker had advised—which had led him to speak further of Jesus as being immaterial, subjective, disembodied, and most of all, experienced as grace only by works of meditation—had gone unremarked without deflecting from the favorable impression made by his opening statement against regulation. Longshot was clearly pleased with his apparent reception and thanked the members for choosing Star-Cross as a place of meeting where they could really feel at home. He then expressed his regrets for having to absent himself so quickly because of another commitment and turned the program over to Ferdie for a video presentation of scenes from the Sacred Garden that he and Tucker had produced solely for this meeting. As background music they had replaced all mantra chants with a recording obtained by Batson of the Emmaus Church Gospel Choir's rendition of the gospel favorite, *I Come to the Garden Alone*, carefully excising the words of the final verse, "I'd stay in the garden with Him . . . but He bids me go through the voice of woe His voice to me is calling," which to Longshot's unaccustomed ear had sounded potentially too diversionary given the video's fund raising purpose.

Longshot had agreed that for this one special occasion the carefully concealed two words, *Of Gethsemane,* in the title of the Sacred Garden's entrance marker as commissioned by Mildred Castleton, that he had from the start directed to be completely positioned out of sight behind surrounding foliage, be brought out into the full light of day and given a single moment in the sun just long enough for the video filming before being quickly turned back again and obscured once more from public view.

When the scheduled time arrived for the two student presentations, Batson introduced them as representatives of the kind of Gospel teaching to be found at Star-Cross. Both he and Tucker felt a sense of pride in their students whose demeanor was at once respectful of the audience, and yet unhesitating in a willingness to share their personal convictions as to what the texts assigned to them had to say about "doing the Father's business."

The first spoke to the prayer group's favorite, "Know you not that I must be about my Father's business?" (*Lk.* 2:49). This text provided the rationale for business itself to which the Christian executives in highlighting these words of the King James translation of 1611 had become accustomed in reaffirming their Christian capitalism slogan, *His Business is Our Business,* "business" being emphasized as the key term. The problem was, as Tucker and Batson well knew, that in the original Greek of the Gospel text there is no explicit reference to "business," and both had been intent to see if, and how, their student would address this possibly contentious, not to mention in this setting fiscally unproductive, issue.

To her credit, as Tucker would later report in a brief synopsis requested by Longshot, she followed in gist the exegetical steps of reflecting upon the text in its contexts as studied in Batson's courses, but in a fresh and engaging manner that was independently thoughtful and devoid of academic jargon. Urging first a careful listening to the Gospel story itself, she imaginatively detailed *Luke*'s account of Jesus as a boy of twelve, going with his parents in a group of travelers up from their hometown of Nazareth to Jerusalem at the festival time of Passover who is discovered missing on the return trip by his anxious parents, only to be found after three days of searching, sitting in the temple among the teachers, listening and asking them questions, and responding to his distressed parents' concern when they come looking for him by asking, "Did you not know that I must be about my Father's business?"

She then quite gently questioned how this passage sounds when heard in its original language, observing that the word "business" does not explicitly appear there but only much later in a translation from the King James Version of 1611. Observing that the exact original wording is, "Did you not know that I must be in *this* of my father?," with the object of "*this*" left undesignated, she cited the history of commentary evidence to show how most translators take the word "*this*" to imply "this temple," a reference to "this" actual place where Jesus is discovered actively listening and questioning the teachers. Therefore most translations of the verse read, "Did you not know that I must be in my father's *house*?," supplying the additional term "*house*," a term also not coming from the original text by itself but from hearing it in association with references to the temple in the broader context of the Gospel where Jesus is reported to speak of the temple and its activity as being "my Father's house" in that it is a "house of prayer."

We are thus led, Tucker reported the first student testifying, to ask what distinguishes the temple activity in which the boy Jesus is discovered as doing "the Father's business" and what does not? Apparently, it is not the activity of money changers whose primary business concern is commercial and making a profit and whose rate of exchange in effect devalues the poor widow's mite (*Lk.* 21:1–4), thereby turning the Father's house of prayer into a den a robbers. (*Matt.* 21:12–13, *Mk.* 11:15–17, quoting the prophecy of *Is.* 56:7 and *Jer.* 7:1 1, and *John* 2:14–16). Not what the Apostle Paul refers to in writing to the Corinthians as being a "peddler," or "profiteer," of God's Word (*2Cor.* 2:17) in contrast to being a faithful "steward of the mysteries" (*2Cor.* 2:1). And with the distinction clearly drawn and carefully referenced between what she called "the prophetic" in contrast to "the profitable" understanding of "doing the Father's business" the first student speaker, so Tucker approvingly conveyed to Longshot, modestly concluded her impressive presentation with a polite bow to her audience.

He did not divulge that she did so to a bare smattering of perfunctory applause, nothing comparable to that earlier given to Longshot.

The second student testimony appeared equally commendable in Tucker's and Batson's eyes, and Tucker sought to convey as much in his report to Longshot. There was no doubt that the hearing given to the assigned words of *Luke* 19:23, "Why did you not put my money in the bank and collect interest?," could be shown to sound quite different depending upon its different contexts. In this second presentation the student began by inviting the listeners in the room first to reflect upon the most likely present day hearing, then how the reported saying of Jesus sounded in relation to other sayings in the Gospel, and finally how our hearing of this passage today compares up against some currently less detected sounds that inhere in the passage's original setting. Though his language was discreet, and the student communicated his testimony in a manner more indirect than assertive, causing Tucker in a whisper to Batson to ask if he had been feeding him Kierkegaard, what Tucker jotted down in his notes as the gist of his remarks was unmistakably a controversial conclusion. Beginning with the admission that Jesus' words might certainly be heard today as a page from the maxims of Benjamin Franklin's *Poor Richard's Almanack* regarding the benefits of compound interest, the student pointed to notes in the parable's original passage suggesting that the one Jesus describes as a nobleman going forth to seek his own kingdom in a far country and giving the servants in his employ pounds to trade with until he returns is not a Jesus figure doing his Father's business. Precisely the opposite, he is described in the text as someone "hated," of whom those under him are "afraid," and seen as "severe," "reaping what he did not sow," getting rich off other peoples' labor, and then seeking to slay those he considers his enemies.

"Therefore," so Tucker hastily recorded *verbatim* on his cell phone the student's closing remarks, "the startling message I had not expected to hear coming from this text is a reversal of what we may tend to assume to be faithfulness today in doing the Father's business. It is *not* by investing in such market capitalism as in the case of the nine servant majority in this parable who gain the corrupt nobleman's approval. Precisely the reverse, it is the refusal on the part of the one non-complying servant to invest for unjust profit in this manner that surprisingly reveals a truly faithful doing of the Father's business."

This time there was no applause, just dead silence and a quick thank you from the presiding officer who then abruptly announced that their benedictory hymn while donations were being collected would be changed from *Blest Be The Tie That Binds*—which speaks of "the fellowship of kindred minds," Batson whispered to Tucker—to the more militant battle cry of *Onward Christian Soldiers Marching As To War*.

Episode 28

The Donations Arrive

THE PRAYER BREAKFAST HAD come and gone with little notice on the largely abandoned Star-Cross campus since no classes were currently in session. Most students had left for vacation jobs or travel, and Tucker and Batson were anxious for the two student presenters to receive their needed five hundred dollar awards as soon as possible without having to wait unduly. Whether the Christian business association would recognize the diligence of the student efforts and value the genuineness of their testimonial convictions both professors had doubts, given the lukewarm reception accorded them, but they were of one mind that each speaker had fulfilled the difficult assignment in an exemplary manner, bringing great credit to the scholarship of which Star-Cross's students of the Bible were capable, call it *Comparative Hegemonics* or whatever.

With each passing day Longshot had grown more apprehensive awaiting the association's judgment. "I hope they don't think that they can keep us in suspense as if on trial awaiting a possible verdict of capital punishment," Longshot had several times remarked with irritation, though Tucker and Ferdie agreed that for Longshot the situation was exactly that. "But, I ask you, could they not have the courtesy to let me hear something about the total of contributions to expect, knowing that I have a school budget to underwrite?"

That had been over a month ago, and Longshot was now beside himself. Therefore it came as a relief to the three concerned when a summons for Tucker, Ferdie, and Batson called them to an urgent meeting in the President's office. When they assembled Longshot triumphantly held up two unopened certified letters that had just arrived, one addressed to him and the other to Batson with instructions to pass it on to the two students.

"Colleagues," he beamed, "I wanted each of you to be here with me so that we could celebrate our seminary's good fortune together. If I wasn't such an abstainer I would have arranged for a champagne toast all around, but you three can have that later without me. We pulled this off together, so we should rejoice as one in our accomplishment for Star-Cross's benefit. Each of us played a necessary part."

Handing Batson the envelope with the financial awards for the two students, Longshot then unsealed his own. It contained an official looking document embossed with *Business By the Bible Prayer Associates, Inc.* which formally expressed appreciation to the President for hosting a meeting of the association and stated regret that the total amount of donations collected, while hopefully enough to cover most of the seminary's catering expenses for the fifty-three members in attendance, had been less than anticipated. Two reasons for the disappointing result were given. First, the membership had felt that both of the student testimonies had been informed by an anti-capitalist bias prevalent throughout liberal academia today. Second, the prayer breakfast had found the appearance of a statue of a pagan idol in the seminary's *Garden of Gethsemane* video to be a shocking display of blasphemy it could not support. A check was enclosed for twelve hundred thirty-two dollars and seventy-five cents, an outrage Longshot fumed, with a note attached saying that an additional contribution promised from the Doolittles had not been received at the time of mailing but would be sent independently.

Longshot was clearly shaken by such a devastating outcome and asked how this negative turn of events could have occurred so quickly as soon as he had left the meeting, especially since his own welcoming remarks had been given such a positive reception. His Board Chairwoman had led him to expect a possible total of donations in the range of nearly a thousand dollars per attendee, and now these praying mantis business bastards weren't even picking up their breakfast check! How could Ferdie and Tucker have overlooked the photo of the Buddha statue and failed to delete it from their video of the Sacred Garden? How could Tucker have sent him such glowing compliments about the two students' now apparently disastrous presentations? Talk about losing the keys to the Kingdom, had Tucker completely lost his senses as to what their whole enterprise had been about? Who was he trying to deceive?

And turning directly to Batson, Longshot asked if he had not been told that the one and only thing he was mainly responsible for was seeing to it that the testimonies of the two chosen students were truly evangelical?

"I think they were, Sir," Batson replied calmly.

"You do, do you?," Longshot shot back. "Well, we had a lot riding on this, and it's obvious that the message the group got was not what it was expecting to hear."

"That, Sir," Batson said, "is what I take `truly evangelical' to mean."

Both Tucker and Ferdie defended their younger colleague, but it was Batson's comment that spoke for itself, and they all would remember.

As tensions eased Longshot offered his apologies for allowing his extreme disappointment to be voiced in such an accusatory fashion. With a handshake all around and a pat on Batson's shoulder which suddenly seemed broader than ever before the group dispersed, with Tucker and Batson contacting the student presenters to meet them in Tucker's office for the awarding at last of their much deserved and needed honoraria.

The students had been clearly heartened by the approval of their teachers and in arriving expressed again their gratefulness for having been chosen for the opportunity afforded them as they opened their award envelopes.

This time there was no personal letter enclosed—and unbelievably no checks! Just two undesignated gift coupons from the *Business By The Bible Prayer Associates Inc.* each good for five hundred dollars worth of purchases from their list of approved publications which consisted of century old polemics against Darwinian anti-creationist modernism, instructional guides on guaranteed strategies for soul-winning, tracts on the Christian's duty to oppose governmental interference in free markets, and an assortment of books with titles such as *Taking the Bible at its Word—Literally.*

Episode 29

Batson and Angelica Go Sleuthing in Atlanta

WHAT WAS NORMAL FOR Star-Cross was always hard to say, but with the passing of weeks and the approach of a new academic year things relatively had gotten back to something resembling it following the prayer breakfast debacle to raise quick money at the start of the summer. The two students who had been promised awards of five hundred dollars each for making testimonial presentations had eventually been compensated with funds Longshot solicited from the Board of Directors, whose Chair had come through with a significant contribution for the establishment of a *Doolittle Sacred Garden Enhancement Endowment* that would be diverted to meet the seminary's more immediate budgetary needs. Work on the garden labyrinth was nearing completion, and Ferdie had been given the go ahead to place the order for the memorial monument. A sudden unanticipated upsurge in new student admission applications mid-summer that coincided with the timing of other schools and seminaries sending out their rejection slips had meant that, given the fluidity of Star-Cross's non-exclusive acceptance policy, a larger than usual incoming fall class size seemed assured. Tucker and Batson who had borne the brunt of Longshot's blaming for the failure of his devious fund raiser had determined not to nurse a grievance and were relieved just to be able to keep their distance from the President's office during the vacation break and be free to turn their attention to other matters. Among the most important of these was the still outstanding question of Batson's interest in the possibility of pursuing some part time working connection with the refugee mission program in Atlanta that Mildred Castleton's Christmas donation letters had inspired him vocationally to consider.

Tucker felt he could no longer withhold from his junior colleague his suspicions about the program and over several long conversations had divulged to Batson's promise of confidentiality and astonished fascination the facts of Wisteria Dean's and Brother John's past encounters with the seminary—carefully omitting the more sensational details. Now that both were apparently using the same Atlanta post office box with the initials CRAP in soliciting charitable donations the mystery had deepened.

"But who else is aware of all this?," had been Batson's immediate reaction, respecting Tucker's insistent caution not to jump to conspiracy theories with unsubstantiated conclusions, yet suddenly alarmed at the prospect of Mildred Castleton's larcenous betrayal. They agreed between them that Batson was the one first to follow up on his earlier conversations with the generous lady to learn if she was still contributing to the supposed mission or had a location address for it where he might speak personally with someone and find out more details if he made a quick trip to Atlanta.

Batson had hoped for an excuse to visit Atlanta and see Angelica Blankchek who through friends of Professor Broadside had gotten a summer job there working at the university library's Ancient Religions desk. She had sent him a post card that he kept at home on his dresser, to "Dear Professor Batson," saying she was enjoying her vacation time there but missed her friends at Star-Cross and adding that if he ever was in Atlanta to please drop in and say hello. Spurred on by this new opportunity Batson had lost no time in scheduling a visit with Mrs. Castleton who greeted him warmly but acknowledged regretfully that she had received no responses from Wisteria Dean regarding the refugee program to which she had regularly continued to donate and did not have any address for it other than a post office box. "I am sure they must be very busy caring for the children," she explained, "and it's best they not use their limited funds on correspondence." The dear lady did, however, take Batson's interests seriously and arranged for him to make inquiry with her blessing of the legal advisors at the Castleton Trust who upon being made aware of their own lack of information on the subject asked Batson to inform them without delay what his trip was able to discover.

After getting in touch with Angelica and explaining that the professional reason for his trip was to look up a refugee missions center upon the recommendation of their friend Mrs. Castleton who had only a post office address for it in Atlanta and hoped he could find out its actual location in the city, Angelica expressing her surprised delight at hearing from him took down the name *Children's Refugee Assistance Program* and agreed to investigate the resources at the university for any information regarding its local whereabouts. Batson would do his own research online, and they decided to meet on a day when Angelica would have some free time off so that they could explore around town together any leads they might have come up with. "This sleuthing together sounds like fun," Angelica had texted him, "I can hardly wait!"

Batson was not surprised when neither of their searches had been able to come across a refugee program center under what he now had become convinced was an assumed name, and in further exchanges with Angelica she had reported that the name Wisteria Dean also could not be found in any of the university library's records. Like Batson himself, Angelica had not been at Star-Cross during Dean's ill-fated interim and knew nothing of the individual or the circumstances of her dismissal. Keeping his promise of confidentiality to Tucker, Batson related none of the undisclosed suspicious details about Dean to Angelica, but simply observed that Mrs. Castleton had mentioned this name as the one she had been directed to use in mailing her donations.

The day of Batson's arrival in Atlanta was picture perfect with cloudless blue skies overhead, low humidity, and the university grounds still abloom in the flowers of late summer. It was an ideal day for parking the car in an area and walking, and after a quick tour of the library where she worked and the campus surrounding it Angelica gave directions to the parts of the city where several known refugee relief centers were listed as having local offices. Going from one to another Batson and Angelica had gathered to their mutual interest informative material about refugee assistance both at home and abroad currently being provided by agencies of the United Nations, the U. S. Office of Refugee Settlement, the International Rescue Committee, as well as a number of faith communities and secular organizations that cooperated across a wide spectrum.

But nowhere had their inquiries turned up any information regarding an Atlanta based so-called *Children's Refugee Assistance Program.*

Expressing her disappointment at failing to help him obtain the address information that Mrs. Castleton had hoped Batson's trip might secure, Angelica over dinner prior to Batson's departure nevertheless repeated how much pleasure she had gotten from their day of exploring. Emboldened by the glow of toasting their blue sky day together Batson summoned the courage to ask if he might take a selfie of themselves at the restaurant, but Angelica had demurred, a right decision given seminary policy Batson's brain told him, but a let down to his heart.

Quickly changing the topic Batson asked Angelica if in her work at the library's Ancient Religions desk she had ever heard of a *Center of Religious Assessment Policies* that he thought might also possibly be located in Atlanta. "Oh, you mean Brother John?," she exclaimed. "He's the director, and he often comes in to check on things in the stacks. He is a very colorful figure and actually is scheduled to give a talk at the university at the end of summer school promoting the work of his assessment center. It's really incredible that you asked because Brother John has extended an invitation to me and several of my women co-workers not only to come to his lecture but to be his personal guests at a reception following that is being hosted by his center. I can't wait to tell Professor Broadside about meeting such an academic celebrity," Angelica added. "I am sure she will be quite excited."

Hearing from Batson that he himself was not personally acquainted with the director or his center except by reputation, but would like to be able to contact him professionally, Angelica eagerly volunteered to look up Brother John's address in their library records and forward it to him right away.

So their evening ended, admittedly in what mattered most to Batson one of the most blissful days of his summer, and in a hurriedly texted update to Tucker just before leaving Atlanta he risked sharing with his trusted mentor Angelica's appealing comment about the fun of their spending time exploring together and how the pleasure of walking the streets with him had made her feel like a "sleuth"—only to learn later to his acute mortification from Tucker, who promised never to tell, that his mobile device's autocorrection in a gross misreading of street walking had transmitted "sleuth" as "slut."

Episode 30

A New School Year Brings New Vocational Certifications

WITH THE INFLUX OF the new late-applicant entering students for whom Star-Cross had not been their first choice, and who had in most cases reluctantly registered only after being rejected at schools they had hoped to attend, the seminary found itself at the beginning of a new academic year faced with an institutional dilemma. How could its *pan-pneumatic* program, on which Star-Cross was seeking to base its claim to distinctiveness from all traditional religious and theological exclusivisms, accommodate a decidedly particularist vocational commitment on the part of some of its students? In short, someone claiming a call to preach the Gospel? Student orientation sessions had revealed significant disparities among the new arrivals in their college backgrounds and most notably as well in the fact that even a few openly declared that their primary interest in getting a seminary degree was to seek church ordination. This raised instant alarm in the faculty that allowing for such a sectarian career interest would result in the debasement of Star-Cross's *pan-pneumatic* uniqueness by violating its "spiritual but not religious" intentions.

The situation had become complicated by a newly invigorated Board of Directors' announced decision to honor Mildred Castleton by granting increased scholarship aid to all needy students provided that their "vocational goal," so the citation stipulated, "most exemplifies the Spirit of Love from A to Z in keeping with Mrs. Castleton's chapel memorial to her father, Major Thomas Castleton." Longshot had taken this impromptu decision by the Board as a personal affront, since he had not been consulted and had relied on Daphne Doolittle to raise additional money from her fellow Board members as he had requested, but for quite another purpose.

At the faculty's planning day of work before classes began there was general agreement in reaffirming the seminary's earlier position that at Star-Cross spirituality was not to be equated with religion. This view was especially strong among the transitional part-time instructors whose course material tended to be drawn almost entirely from social media and current Internet sites. But differences remained as to what the word spirituality should stand for in the curriculum with one side arguing for "whatever one reverences" that was disputed by another side as being too objectifying and insisting instead on "reverencing as such," which in turn was countered as too subjectifying, only to be met by yet a third side's dismissal that the whole subject/object dichotomy was simply an imposition of binary Western thinking. Disagreements mainly came down to whether one tended to think of the word spirituality more existentially in terms of "the divine within" or more metaphysically, as some expressed it, or anti-metaphysically as others contended, of an "ultimate beyond," insisting on beyond form, beyond identity, even beyond any specificity of divinity or of consequence. A most convenient excuse Tucker would think to himself in his more cynical moments for trying to justify one's teaching of inconsequence. He was glad there was no such word in the New Testament.

Interrupting this discussion, a sudden clatter of noise from an adjoining room on the hall sent a messenger to silence the disturbance who returned to report that an innocent group of new students unaware that a faculty meeting was taking place was clapping and singing *He's Got The Whole World In His Hands.*

"Jesus Christ, what in God's name are we coming to?," one of the most ardent anti-religionists on the faculty heatedly complained, obviously unburdened by vocabulary consistency.

A suggestion of first inquiring of the four curricular areas to see what courses were presently being offered that might conceivably be tailored more specifically to meet the needs of those students expressing particularist vocational aims without violating the seminary's *pan-pneumatic* commitments proved futile when no one risked being accused pedagogically of religious privileging, and even one of the most compliant and unexceptional members of the Comparative Hegemonics faculty was implicitly ridiculed, much to Tucker's distain, by being questioned as to whether a listed seminar comparing *Quotations from Mao Tse-Tung's Little Red Book* with *Sarah Baker Eddy's Science and Health With Key to the Scriptures* would in fact be bias free.

It was then that members of the Experiential Modalities and Practices area proposed that the problem of vocational diversity be considered as a practical matter of equipping students with career certifications rather than as compromising the theoretical guidelines governing Star-Cross's current curriculum. The college records of the entering class showed that some of the applicants who cited their particular vocational motivations actually had overall grade averages higher than those who did not. Thus it was proposed that by instituting a new policy of career certifications the seminary could address not only the particular vocational concerns presented by the entering class but also the longer standing problem of better assisting graduates with Star-Cross degrees to find job placements. While not everyone found the idea persuasive, the faculty did consent to divide into discussion groups to think through the details, not of what such a proposal would mean, so its advocates instructed, but of how it would work.

When sufficient time for deliberation had been given and the faculty had reassembled, it was clear that the certification idea had gained support with most apprehensions allayed. The "parochials," as some faculty members initially had disparagingly referred to them, would only be assigned to advisers willing to take them and desirous of working with them. Academic requirements would be the same as for everyone else, with the only difference being that students applying for a *Spiritual Practitioner Certification Award*, as it would be called, would be allowed to substitute the credit for one course in each of their three years by fulfilling a two-fold obligation in a manner approved by the faculty to self-initiate a program with the necessary resources to work toward their vocational goal and to maintain a personal website for reporting and reflecting upon their progress.

Upon a recommendation by Tucker it was unanimously voted that money from the new Castleton Scholarship Fund could be drawn upon by deserving applicants in financing their self-initiated certification projects as long as these complied with the Board's stipulation that only those vocational aims that most exemplified "the Spirit of Love from A to Z in keeping with Mrs. Castleton's chapel memorial to her father, Major Thomas Castleton" would qualify for such awards. This advantage, it was agreed, would assure that such an accommodation for those students with particularist vocational commitments would not violate Star-Cross's *pan-pneumatic* policy of non-exclusiveness.

By the completion of registration, while only a relative few of the incoming students had been certain enough of their vocational commitments to enroll in the certification program, it had met with general acceptance. Three of the declared students would be preparing for church ordination, while the rest, some ten or so who were still formulating their proposals, varied in career intentions that were for the most part related to some form of advanced yoga instruction and spiritual retreat directorship, with one additional specialization in sacred gardening.

Overall academic performance at Star-Cross had shown definite improvement in recent semesters, as acknowledged in accreditation monitoring reports. There were fewer students applying for *Low Interest Quotient* exemptions from grading now that the required *LIQ* medical endorsements, fraudulently signed wholesale during the interim administration of Wisteria Dean with the postmortem use of the deceased Dr. Wetmore Readily's signature stamp from his livelier days as the once venerable seminary physician, were no longer available. On a brighter note several highly qualified members of the senior class who were of comparable academic caliber to Angelica Blankchek and the two New Testament presenters who had spoken at the business executives' prayer breakfast had indicated their intentions to apply to Ph.D. programs following their seminary graduation.

With the approval of the *Spiritual Practitioner Certification Awards* Longshot, eager as always to capitalize on any innovation, had his office prepare an immediate press release, prompting alarmed Humane Society officials to call for an investigation following its headline in the local news, **STAR-CROSS SEMINARY IN AN SPCA INITIATIVE APPROVES THE ISSUING OF DOGMA LICENSES.**

Episode 31

Professor Schmoot's Resolve to Refocus Priorities

Professor T. Upton Schmoot, as he preferred to be known professionally—as opposed to Tucker U. Schmoot, a name passable in print but impossible for a spoken introduction—had long recognized that he was not given to obvious enthusiasms. This was the case both academically and with respect to religion. In his teaching he tended to be unimpressed by the latest fads, viewing the job seeking market of academia as a cacophony of sycophants. Yet in a choice between defending establishments or supporting new alternatives he more often than not appeared to side with those focused upon the unprecedented, a perspective he liked to think to himself that was more aligned with the usually misunderstood significance of New Testament apocalyptic. When annually he attended the ten thousand or so member conventions of *The American Academy of Religion* he was never sure where he belonged in the cacophony, joining Batson and other colleagues part of the time in the biblical sections more related to his own field, then leaving to sit in on the theological and religious studies discussion sections that seemed worlds apart, greeting other colleagues and friends there, yet all the while not really being at home in either.

With respect to religion, and more personally to his own beliefs, he also defied conventional labeling. While he valued the Christian creeds of his high Church tradition as liturgical expressions, his interest in them and in the traditional cadences of *The Book of Common Prayer* was more aesthetic than doctrinal. He had become an infrequent churchgoer turned off by the clericalism. As for dogmatic controversies over orthodoxy his unspoken attitude ranged from boredom to a plague on all your houses. There were better things to do with one's time. In this regard Tucker fit well at Star-Cross. Yet he found the arrogance of the seminary's more stridently anti-religionist faculty members as distasteful as it was superficial, and though his differing worship experiences from occasional visits to various congregations in his capacity as a seminary professor never failed to elicit his genuine respect, he always left church knowing he was only a visitor.

But now the recent seminary deliberations over student vocational commitments along with his conversations with Batson over his young colleague's sense of mission had raised the question of his own commitments to a level of consciousness he had not been faced with before. In some of the twilight evenings when he could get away alone for a drive along the isolated back country roads that he found most hospitable for introspection he reflected on years past when still struggling to come to terms with the painful failure of his marriage he had once self-mockingly characterized himself to his therapist, saying, "When I was young I avoided New Year's Eve parties for fear someone would want to kiss me at midnight, and as I became older I avoided them for fear no one would." He wasn't much of a party guy. That was for sure. But who he was as someone whose life counted for anything other than avoidance was a question he found much harder to answer. Super Ego or not, he reproached himself for becoming preoccupied with it, a navel gazing stereotype of Jung's mid-life second identity crisis, he would tell himself, that was in his case just somewhat delayed, but none the less inhibiting.

One thing he could not deny was that he cared about his students and felt most energized when concentrating upon the current opportunities of teaching the New Testament and furthering the quality of scholarship generally in a seminary such as Star-Cross. Each year found his incoming classes eager to dispute traditional appeals to scriptural authority, and more and more this challenge of authority had come to have its secular counterparts in society at large. The question *Who's to Say?* was not confinable to an arcane academic concern relevant only to biblical studies. Two of the most contested social issues of the day, authority and trust, had their prototype in such studies. Engaging this current situation with classes in his occupation as a New Testament teacher, whatever its frustrations, was a gift he treasured, even if he was not ready to speak of a calling. He resolved to refocus his priorities with greater consistency to it.

To this aim the new student vocational certifications provided him with an immediate opportunity for responding more readily to individual requests seeking his advisement. A prime instance occurred when one of the newer students who had expressed an intent at registration to prepare for ministerial ordination asked to consult with him regarding Star-Cross's policy of requiring inclusive language in all references to deity. Tucker's first impulse was to suspect that the individual wanted an exemption from the seminary's long held academic standards against gender privileging, a request for which he could muster no sympathy. To his surprise such was not the case. Far from encountering as anticipated a closed mind and possibly belligerent attitude on the subject, Tucker was impressed by the obvious efforts of the student to understand and comply conscientiously with an unfamiliar requirement. Thus with empathy for the student who as a recently hired church youth leader had asked if the professor would please read over remarks prepared for a talk the coming Sunday to see if the language was acceptably inclusive, Tucker, having done so, very considerately suggested, so as not to embarrass, that even when preparing to speak of God in our talks inclusively, not simply with use of the masculine pronoun alone, but as in this case "*She/He/It*," it is always important to first read aloud to ourselves what we have written in order to hear how it may sound to the ear of our audience before delivering it.

Two opportunities for becoming more supportive of faculty colleagues had to do with the "publish or perish" demands of academia. Tucker's own publications were not extensive, but they had received good critical reviews, and his best selling *Parallels in Sacred Writings* had become a standard textbook in its field. He determined not to neglect his own scholarly projects but to become more available to his associates in promoting interest in their projects as well.

In the first instance he set aside more time in his schedule for continuing discussions with Batson on the progress of revising his dissertation. Catchy titles had remained a hurdle in a market driven more by notoriety than by content. One publisher after merely seizing upon a brief reference in Batson's manuscript to *Revelation* 3:20, "If anyone hears my voice and opens the door, I will come in and sup with him," had even insisted on the title, *Guess Who's Coming to Supper?* Several others objected to the authoritarian implications associated with the concept of revelation, such as the denial of freedom of thought. "Exactly the opposite of what the book is about," Batson and Tucker had agreed. The authority question in the New Testament was the question of the authoring of freedom. With Tucker's encouragement Batson had undertaken a further consolidation of his dissertation argument to highlight this one crucial point. Entitling this new effort to characterize the God of the New Testament revealed in Jesus Christ as *The Author of Freedom* he had submitted a précis to yet another publisher and had this time been granted a publishing contract with the only proviso that the title be changed to *The Author of Liberty* in order to call to the public's mind the generally familiar revered expression of "our fathers' God to Thee, Author of liberty" from the fourth verse of *My Country Tis of Thee* and thereby give the book, in the editor's words, "a more popular and patriotic sales appeal."

In a second and quite unexpected instance which required more of his time, but which gratified him greatly, Professor Broadside had sought his help in dealing with a complicated turn of events of immense personal urgency. To update her academic dossier she needed without delay to meet a deadline for having more current publications. An egregious publishing error just over a year ago involving her most recent spiritual meditations recorded on her lute for an international meeting of Buddhist peace seekers had mistaken her carefully chosen title *Luten Meditations* for *Lenten Meditations* which forced a recall at considerable revenue loss preventing reissue of all the two hundred copies bearing the misprinted cover, *Lenten Meditations for Peace Seeking Buddhists, With Floppy Disk.* Since this set-back she had worked steadily on a paper to present on "The Nuns of St. Fabula" at the next *American Academy of Religion* sessions of the Reconstructing Herstory work group of which she was an active member. As fate would have it, and in this happenstance Tucker could only concur with Isadora's feeling that fate indeed was against her, another *AAR* study group had been scheduled at the same hour on the emerging cultural phenomenon in the news of the increasing number of students and other Americans checking the "none of the above" box when asked to indicate their religious affiliation or preference, thus acquiring in social media the designation of "the Nones." By a most bizarre mix-up of word play confusion Isadora's paper topic on "The Nuns of St. Fabula" had apparently been assigned by mistake for discussion in the so-called Nones Phenomenon Study Group where it had become listed for delivery on that group's program schedule as "The Nones of St. Fabula."

Informed of the historical research Broadside had done, and sensitive to his colleague's acute personal dilemma now that her meeting deadline was fast approaching, Tucker urged that she not cancel her paper's announced presentation as scheduled but instead use the play on words in her title as a means of adapting her research on the Amazon Sisters to illustrate specific issues pertinent to the cultural rise of the Nones. There were a number of self-designating Nones in the Star-Cross student body, some promoting the T shirt label proudly, as well as in the faculty itself. The material was definitely there for a creative revamping into an insightful case study.

In subsequent consultations Tucker gave attentive consideration to Isadora's analysis of the significance of spiritual anti-institutionalization and resistance to affiliation, exemplified by the Amazon Sisters of St. Fabula, as two of the primary factors in the rise of the Nones as a cultural phenomenon and commended with genuine approval her assessment. "I knew I could count on your understanding and help," his visibly relieved colleague had thanked him. "I will always remember how you came to my aid in seconding the President's proposal of support in our faculty meeting when campus vandals tried to humiliate me by defacing the Buddha in our Sacred Garden with a military helmet and rifle when the visiting peace seekers met here. One never forgets such loyalty."

Tucker kept his promise to be present at the *American Academy of Religion* forum when Isadora gave her paper and inwardly applauded her skill in fielding questions. A final one asked about rumors which had once circulated that some funds bequeathed by the Amazon Sisters to Star-Cross may have become unaccounted for. To this query Broadside had responded forthrightly that to her knowledge such rumors had arisen because of some temporary dislocations due to construction on campus, but that was a subject not within the scope of her paper, but for another day.

Episode 32

"The Subject for Another Day"

THE SUBJECT "FOR ANOTHER day" with which Professor Broadside had successfully defended the focus of her *AAR* presentation in fact arrived sooner than either Tucker or Batson had anticipated, and neither was ready to allow it to rob them of valuable time from their present academic pursuits. Tucker had settled upon a new book proposal outlining the hermeneutical issues at the core of the "fake news" charges and counter charges that had first drawn headlines in the 2016 presidential campaign and election and, with the intriguing title *Fake News and The Good News* questioning the relevance of factuality as the test of truth in either case, had quickly secured a publishing contract.

Batson, for his part, was wasting no time as the new semester weeks passed in readying his revised dissertation on *The Author of Liberty* to meet his own contracted publishing deadlines for completion. Immediately upon returning from his quick trip to Atlanta in the late summer, just prior to the start of the new fall term, he had reported to the legal staff of the Castleton Trust as requested and informed it of his inability to locate any whereabouts for a *Children's Refugee Assistance Program* in that city. The staff had thoroughly sounded out Tucker's suspicions as well, and together both were thanked and assured that their concerns were indeed being looked into.

Angelica shortly before moving back to begin her final year at Star-Cross had notified Batson that a search of library membership records had turned up only a post office box address on file for Brother John and that recent inquiries mailed to it had received no response. She added that as the Summer Session programs were ending at the university a circulated announcement had gone out in the school calendar of events simply stating that the originally scheduled lecture and reception sponsored by the *Center for Religious Assessment Policies* had been postponed until an unspecified future date. No explanation had been given. Busy with the new work load of her graduate year of seminary studies neither she nor Batson had pursued their investigation further. What she had done was bring back from Atlanta additional information regarding refugee assistance programs which had increasingly become a subject of their mutual interest.

But now another one of Longshot's urgent messages had summoned Tucker to come by the President's office as soon as possible, and harnessing his new determination not to let the President's agenda distract him unduly from his own, Tucker went as soon as his classes for the day ended.

"I am speaking to you in total confidence," Longshot began, motioning Tucker to take a seat, "because you are the one person on this faculty that I know I can trust to make sure the financial tightrope balancing act we depend on with the Castleton Trust remains above suspicion. Don't repeat this to anyone, but there has been some snooping recently by the Board into our financial accounts. They have hired outside auditors at the urging, so Doolittle tells me, of the Trust's representative, and are looking at alleged discrepancies in the records, or lack of them, in Wisteria Dean's interim administration during my last sabbatical. They don't say where the allegations are coming from, just another one of these "unnamed sources." I have been emphatic that you and I were in continual contact while I was away in India and saw to it that Dean was quietly allowed to resign for poor book keeping with the understanding that none of this would be made public with any filing of charges on either side to the detriment of the seminary's reputation. Why I suspect this has all come up, Tucker, is that some members of the faculty most antagonistic to Dean's appointment at the time got all exercised by Mildred Castleton's contributions last Christmas in the faculty's name to a refugee children's program recommended by Dean and have spread rumors about school finances to the Castleton Trust. Incidentally, Broadside I hear has been digging around in the reports of false accusations about the mishandling of the Amazon Sisters' reliquary bequest that occurred under Dean's watch and is likely the one who is stirring the kettle in all this. As you and I know she's constantly got her nose to the ground sniffing out any excuse to express outrage. But that's just between us, so please keep this to yourself. I have told the investigators to meet with you apart from my presence as someone closest to Mildred Castleton and knowledgeable about what took place to get this whole misunderstanding quickly straightened out. I wanted to give you a head's up, Tucker, that you will be hearing from them. I know this comes as a shock. You look dumbfounded, and I don't want to alarm you. But just remember you hold the key to getting us all off the hook and preventing our tightrope with the Castleton Trust from breaking because the dear madam believes whatever you tell her."

Tucker upon leaving the President's office did not wait to hear from the Trust legal team but contacted them immediately to let them know that Longshot had advised him to expect a call from them. They confirmed the President's account but told Tucker that their investigations had moved well beyond it with results they expected to wrap up and be able to share confidentially with him and Batson after consulting with members of the Board and Mrs. Castleton within the next couple weeks. When a call did come arranging for Batson and himself to meet with them in the offices of the Castleton Trust the investigators reported that evidence had been established which Longshot himself when confronted had been forced in a sworn statement to admit, though all the while protesting in a codicil his honesty and innocence in so doing as a "postmodern destabilization of meaning" consistent with the fluidity of spiritual testimony.

The facts, as uncovered and verified, were as follows. Longshot had agreed to let Wisteria Dean resign without facing charges over her malfeasance in the mishandling of funds involved in the loss of the Amazon Sisters of St. Fabula reliquary endowment, coupled with the fraudulent withdrawal payments to the deceased Dr. Wetmore Readily for the *Low Interest Quotient* student medical authorizations, on condition that she sign a certified letter of commitment to send him specified amounts of repayment periodically for the foreseeable future until such unaccountable losses incurred during her interim administration had been recouped. This was done to prevent a public scandal causing great harm to the seminary. These payments were then used by Longshot in turn to pay off Brother John who had threatened to sue him for breach of contract and defamation of character in having been rejected as an outside consultant for academic assessment. This recycling of money from Dean to Longshot to Brother John was mainly sourced by funds from Mildred Castleton who had remained unaware of the threefold collaboration to which they were being put but whose most recent Christmas donation letters to the faculty had unknowingly served to reveal. Why Dean and Brother John had thought to avoid detection by using the same Atlanta *CRAP* post office box, Longshot, expressing his surprise, declared not to know. In defense he had argued that since a portion of the money, though when pressed admittedly a minor percentage, had indeed been allocated by him to his ashram in India where indigent refugee children of the area sometimes came seeking donations, Dean's solicitation of aid funds for that purpose could not itself be judged a fraud. Nor, he adamantly maintained, had he committed any legal violation since the expenditures of his office as President were at his sole discretion, and a mere lack of disclosure on his part did not constitute a violation of law.

The briefing concluded by informing Tucker and Batson that at Mildred Castleton's insistence the whole matter for the moment was to be kept strictly secret with only them being made aware of the situation as the ones who had been involved in first bringing the issue to light. In classified consultation with members of the Board the legal team had recommended that the President relinquish office immediately with conspiracy of larceny charges filed against him, Wisteria Dean, and Brother John. But Mrs. Castleton was refusing to consent until she could confer with both of them and, at her explicit request, include the student Angelica Blankchek as well.

Episode 33

An Encounter in the Sacred Garden

Upon returning to campus, Batson having gone his way to contact Angelica, Tucker spotted the President at a distance sitting alone in the Sacred Garden among the lotus plants near the new labyrinth monument to Major Castleton. As he drew nearer Longshot beckoned for him to come join him. For all the seminary's emphasis upon meditation it occurred to Tucker that in their years of academic association they had seldom engaged in it together. He wondered if Longshot knew how much the Trust investigators had just revealed to him, but it quickly became apparent that he did not.

"I have more news that I have wanted to share with you before the rest of the faculty learns about it," Longshot began. "For quite awhile I have been wanting to get out from under so much administrative pressure and assume more of my ashram spirituality leadership. My office staff is practically worthless, with my personal secretary seemingly incapable of issuing a clear press release. And now with the extra snooping going on and all the outside file checkers looking over your shoulder, this strikes me as a good time to make a change. So I paid a visit to our dear lady this week and requested her support for a leave of absence research proposal I am submitting to the Board for their approval. To sweeten the offer I am willing to forego my salary from the seminary while I am away, and—get this, Tucker—I am recommending that you be appointed with full presidential salary to act with title of Interim President during my absence."

"Oh, Byah, no, no!," Tucker interrupted with sudden alarm, calling Longshot by his first name that was almost never used. "You know that is impossible. Teaching is my academic role, and I am neither qualified nor interested in becoming an administrator with you away. What in the world did Mildred Castleton say to all this?"

"Well, Tucker, it should come as no surprise to you that she listened most intently and upon my mention of your name instantly appeared quite favorable to giving further thought to my proposal. As I was leaving, she wished me well and said, 'Mr. President, one thing you and I will always agree on is our confidence in Professor Schmoot.' So now, good colleague, you see you will have more to discuss with the dear lady when you meet with her than you ever may have anticipated, and we can make sure that the Trust lawyers are prevented from influencing her against us."

With that, Longshot resumed his meditative composure, and not wishing either to disturb him further or depart abruptly Tucker without comment turned to the labyrinth and slowly began to walk it as his mind raced in his heightened uncertainty. Batson's unwelcome confession that had so irritated him awhile back of feeling ashamed that he had violated the trust of both Mildred Castleton and Angelica merely by appearing on one occasion to confirm each of them when he knew that their positions differed suddenly dogged his mind. He had not forgotten his young colleague's response when he had thought Batson should lighten up and not take himself so seriously, "You don't know how unworthy it feels to be deceptive." My God, he had thought at the time, the unknowing innocence of youth! It would take more than a pizza party now to get him through this new morass.

Despite all his objections to various ideas and actions of Longshot through the years of his presidency, and a suppressed resentment at being a ploy for his purposes, Tucker had persuaded himself that his complicity was for the greater good of Star-Cross. For all its seeming craziness to Western sensibilities the President had sought to instill an ethos that gave the place a unique character among the more traditional seminaries that was worth defending. At their best its *pan-pneumatic* aspirations enabled a multi-cultural diversity and respect for equal rights that was well ahead of its time. In the words of Tucker's favorite ode by Robert Burns the seminary provided no settlement for the "Rigidly Righteous," either of the right or the left, and no camp grounds for narcissistic soul saving whether by works or by grace. In his own field of scriptural interpretation Tucker had been emboldened by the resistance to the literalistic claims of any Bible quoting fundamentalism, not only in its academically discredited exclusivist conservative forms, but also in the less acknowledged and equally exclusivist liberal forms of a literalistic atheist fundamentalism as well. The individual nearby now besieged, positioned alone in contemplation among his beloved lotus plants, was notwithstanding the one who had maneuvered the hardest for years to see that the resources of the Castleton Trust not abandon the promise of the struggling Star-Cross endeavor.

Silently leaving the labyrinth walk, but not the continuing turmoil in his brain as to what would be coming next, Tucker departed the Sacred Garden as the sun was beginning to set and headed home across campus. He wondered how much of Longshot's story of his going to see Mrs. Castleton was factual, and if so had she in turn reported any of the details to her lawyers of the Castleton Trust? Could that be the reason she was reportedly withholding her consent to follow her own legal investigative team's recommendations? What her requested meeting with Batson, Angelica, and himself could contribute to the situation, or what the dear lady would be counting on him to do, was not evident to him. For a long time in quite uncharacteristic fashion he thumbed through the pages of his Greek New Testament unsure if he was meditating or superstitiously praying for an epiphany until at a late night hour, still at a loss and searching, he turned off the light and fell into a fitful sleep.

Episode 34

The Dear Lady Decides

THE NEXT DAY BROUGHT word from the Trust legal advisers that Mrs. Castleton would be most desirous to meet with Professors Schmoot and Belfry and Miss Blankchek at an agreeable time that did not interfere with any of their class schedules. This would be a business meeting at which she wished to seek their personal counsel and which would require their complete confidentiality. Instead of coming to her home this time she asked that they gather along with several of her staff in the office conference room of the Castleton Trust. Clearly this was not to be simply an afternoon tea or a sherry hour.

By the end of the week, with no class conflicts, a time was set, and the meeting convened with Mrs. Castleton in the convener's chair. Tucker was struck with the charitable woman's capacity. She had not presided over an inherited family fortune of benefaction for nearly half a century for nothing, he reflected, and though in recent years she had become more reliant upon assistance for her hearing and vision, and increasingly accepted the help of a steadying arm on public occasions when walking or standing, the Old Major's daughter at the center of the table before him now was clearly in charge with her sense of responsibility undiminished.

He could imagine the dismay at the disclosures at hand that must lie beneath her resoluteness as she cordially welcomed and introduced each person present before turning with a courteous smile to ask Dr. Belfry if he would first please lead them in a word of prayer. To Tucker's relief and Angelica's fascination Batson responded briefly and with a reserve appropriate for the occasion. This was not revival hour, but consistent with a Castleton agenda.

A summary report from one of the Trust investigators was next requested which contained essentially the facts that Tucker and Batson had previously been given with the exception of the one addition that the two individuals engaged in collaboration with President Longshot had been traced through a tip to their recently acquired new employment and given their statements as well. The individual known as Brother John had lately sought and gained a contract, along with Dr. Wisteria Dean as his professional assistant, to become chief spiritual analyst to the *Business By The Bible Prayer Associates,* an organization of wealthy corporate executives dedicated to safeguarding Christian capitalistic values in American higher education.

"I don't recall ever hearing of this organization," Mildred Castleton commented offhandedly, as Tucker and Batson exchanged uncertain glances but did not interrupt the Trust investigator who hastened on to complete his report that the two individuals in question had reincorporated their joint analytic enterprise as *Christians Reborn And Producing,* leaving the same initials unchanged that identified their Atlanta post office box.

Mildred next asked the group's opinions of what should be their primary consideration in the present situation and listened intently to the ongoing discussion. There was immediate agreement with the legal team's spokesman that the defrauding of Castleton must receive its just penalty. That seemed obvious enough, and to the further question of what is just, his general reply was equally simple. "It's getting what's coming to you, what you deserve."

"And are they the same, do you think?," the convener asked. She was not playing games, and the others gave heed.

"I sure hope not," Batson replied, after an awkward pause as the lawyers looked uncomprehending about what to say. Tucker sensed where the questioning was headed. A fair penalty for the offences committed was demanded by the evidence, but it need not require that President Longshot be destroyed. Castleton's Calvinism had no place for sentimentality when it came to acknowledging transgression, but there was a place for clemency in justice, and that must be respected too. The upshot of the continued discussion was that the good of the seminary should come first which required that if settlements could be negotiated out of court with the sworn statements of each of the three betrayers of trust acknowledging their dereliction of duty under false pretenses there would be no filing of larceny or extortion charges with the attendant damaging publicity. Longshot had taken a similar position in the past with respect to the dismissal of Wisteria Dean. The recommendation of the legal team that the President had forfeited his right to continue in office and should be asked to leave immediately was met only with silence.

Mrs. Castleton who had herself refrained from commenting except for an occasional question, but had followed closely what everyone else present had to say, now expressed her own judgment. "I am so grateful to each of you," she began, "and I concur in most all of your observations. As I have heard you, the discussion seems to have revolved around two questions, whether our primary concern in this troubling matter should be that a just legal penalty be exacted for the admitted misuse of funds, or whether that the good of the seminary and its reputation should be made foremost. There are good reasons in support of both positions, and you have offered them. But for me there is primarily a third that at this moment in our history takes priority over both, and that is the mission to alleviate the suffering of refugee children. Their faces are ever before me. These children must not bear the brunt of increased suffering because of this diversion of funds, inadequate for the need as they have been, but which nevertheless were intended for their benefit. You have convinced me that this is a crime that definitely requires restitution, and equally that concern for the good of the seminary must ever be foremost in our endeavors. In that regard, dear Star-Cross friends, I hope I can also persuade you to approve a proposal that the legal team is aware of that involves a role for each of you. I want to discuss the details with you personally before asking for your decision, and will be in touch with the three of you further in the next few days. In the meantime I am trusting that for the good of everyone this whole matter will remain only among us."

Driving back to campus after bidding their farewells Tucker in jest chided his evangelical colleague that apparently Brother John's "born again" upbringing was proving more lucrative a second time around, commenting dryly, "Quite a twist of fate."

"Or maybe Providence?," Batson kidded. "Or better yet," adding with a wink and a nod at a subdued Angelica, "what the postmodernists like to call a *second naiveté*?"

"I don't think, Sir, that Paul Ricoeur would approve of your use of his term," Angelica returned the tease. She had written an assignment on it in a class with Batson and was still overcome by what she had learned of Brother John during their meeting and even more wondering what Mrs. Castleton would want to discuss with her as well.

Episode 35

Broadside's Bombshell

THE FALL SEMESTER HAD gone quickly, and considering the events it had brought about meant that significant changes were in store for Star-Cross as it headed beyond the winter holidays toward its spring graduation. The marvel was that these events had remained undisclosed to the wider seminary, as Mildred Castleton had urgently requested, and with the forthcoming changes still to be announced in the final weeks of the academic year it appeared that, given the circumstances, the best possible transition for the good of Star-Cross would be achieved. Both President Longshot and Mrs. Castleton each privately credited Tucker, to his intense discomfort, with being the key to this achievement. Neither knew what the other had confided to him.

For his part Longshot was granted an honorable dismissal from his presidency at the end of the academic year that enabled him to portray it as an upcoming leave of absence to establish what he called *Spirituality and Meditation Retreats* overseas. His request that such retreats be designated as *Star-Cross Abroad* had been rejected by the Board of Directors at the instance of the Castleton Trust, along with his further request that the seminary award him the title of *Professsor of Pan-Pneumatic Practice* to enhance his efforts. Clemency did not extend that far. His dismissal from the seminary would carry the stipulation that henceforth he forfeit all rights of association with *Star-Cross* including the hyphenated use of its name. In the coming year after sufficient time had passed his indefinite leave would be announced as permanent. Longshot credited Tucker with influencing Mildred Castleton, as he had requested him, to support his application to the Board for a leave of absence, thinking all the while that Tucker would not know that it would be but a guise for an honorable firing.

For Mildred Castleton's part her decision had prevailed that exacting justice for Longshot's transgressions did not require his reputation's destruction. The President would be allowed to complete the remaining weeks of the school term as if nothing were amiss with Tucker helping out in his office as his yet to be announced replacement. She did not know that Longshot had trusted Tucker with the story, whether erroneous or not, that such was precisely his scheme for finagling a leave of absence by recommending that Tucker be put in charge of the presidential office as the one whose word he knew the dear benefactor would believe could always be relied on.

Subsequent to their initial meeting in the conference room of the Castleton Trust Mildred Castleton had, as promised, followed up with conversations and specific requests to Tucker, Batson, and Angelica. Mindful that Angelica in her graduating year had been disheartened by learning for the first time of some of the reported revelations, she spoke with her first. She wanted Angelica to be certain that the concern for refugee children's relief was indeed to be given priority by the Castleton Trust and to this end she was recommending the appointment of a special assistant to advise her personally in proposing and carrying out this endeavor. Was it not the case, as Professor Belfry had mentioned to her following his trip to Atlanta, that they had a mutual interest in exploring such refugee programs further? And would she, upon her graduation from Star-Cross be interested in assuming such a position, at least until her arrangements for graduate school were definite? The salary would assure that her future academic costs would more easily be covered.

Equally unexpected but no less joyfully received was the Castleton advisory role offered to Batson. As explained to him, a decision had been made to employ a personal consultant in making philanthropic decisions, most particularly those involving donations relating to seminary education and to Star-Cross in particular. In urging him to consider such a position as part of a vocational mission, in addition to his teaching, Mildred gave three reasons that had led her, as she expressed it, to Professor Belfry as her preferred choice. First, his proven dedication to first rate scholarship since coming to Star-Cross had been convincingly attested to her by inquiries of both faculty colleagues and students. Second, he was at home in the faith that had been the founding heritage of Star-Cross but recognized that this faith itself called for one to respect equally those who do not share it.

Or as she put it, "You know the Gospel, but you do not confuse it with those who simply say 'Lord, Lord,'" adding with a wicked twinkle in her eye, "I think the privilege of meeting Miss Blankchek has been good for both of us!" Her third reason was matter-of-fact and to the point, "And we can pray together."

Conversations, for there were more than one, with Tucker had proven more difficult for he definitely did not wish to be appointed as seminary president even for just the interim required until such time could elapse to allow for a permanent successor to be named. It could well take at least a full academic year for the seminary to announce and conduct the search for a presidential replacement, and not the least of the responsibilities that would surely fall to him in the meanwhile would be the delicate orchestrating of the absent Longshot's falsely ostensible decision that the establishing of his *Spirituality and Meditation Retreats* abroad had proven to require his full time commitment. Yet Tucker had to acknowledge with Mildred Castleton that a successful transition without publicized scandal to the detriment of Star-Cross could not be achieved without his willingness to assume at least a transitional leadership role. Further complicating the picture was that Daphne Doolittle, from whose information the Castleton investigators had been able to discover the whereabouts of Brother John and Wisteria Dean, had advised them that she had arranged with Longshot for Overjoy to be the sole supplier of emotional enhancement potions and lotions at his overseas *Spirituality and Meditation Retreats* where stimulants would be less subject to legal restrictions. It was hard to know, Tucker thought, who would be profiting the most from such a deal, with the candle of mutual advantage seeming to be burning at both ends.

Despite his misgivings Tucker had consented to assume this unwelcome responsibility for which he knew Longshot would take credit as being his gift to his erstwhile confidant of a salary increase for filling in while he was on leave, and Mildred Castleton expressed her gratitude for his essential role in enabling the seminary to move on unscathed through a potentially crippling dilemma. The one unexpected good fortune in all this was the rejoicing he shared with Angelica and Batson who eagerly accepted the offers of their new positions.

Without comment the auditing inspectors camping in the President's office had gradually been withdrawn, much to the relief of Longshot's own bewildered staff, their investigative reports to the Castleton Trust having been completed. Campus life had resumed its seasonal pace as the focus turned to preparations for the coming end of the academic year and graduation. The blossoms of the Sacred Garden were responding to Ferdie's loving care in a palette of color that suffused the grounds as an emblem of peace. All this, Tucker said to himself, pausing at the view from his office window, he must take time to notice. It was so worth his defending, and for the moment his lying low.

That moment proved to be short lived as a sudden repeat of an earlier message on his mobile phone requesting to see him from Isadora Broadside that he had left unanswered signaled that any moment of reprieve for Tucker would not be long. She had news, she said, that could not wait regarding rumors of what may have happened to the reliquary endowment funds to the seminary from the Amazon Sisters that she needed to make him aware of as the faculty member she knew she could most trust. Trying not to show his exasperation in his voice, Tucker immediately volunteered to make a trip to her campus office and within the hour had been given the full story.

In breathless haste Broadside informed him that with the help of Rigore Mortisse her research had discovered grounds for surmising that Longshot himself had diverted the reliquary funds and covered up Wisteria Dean's fraud of the Low Interest Quotient medical certification payments. In essence it was clear listening to Broadside's report that Mortisse himself was actually her only evidence. By trailing the examining auditors around the library Mortisse was sure that he had on more than one occasion heard them remark something about the President's "overseas ventures." Checking this out with Longshot's staff when the President was away from his office, Mortisse had secretly gleaned from Longshot's secretary that the President was placing all responsibility upon Tucker for Dean's mishandling of finances while he had been in India on sabbatical and had instructed Tucker back here at home to take care of the matter.

But now, and here Isadora took a deep breath before delivering her bombshell, "Longshot's secretary is certain she heard one of the file examiners whispering something to another about Longshot diverting Castleton funds to set up—can you believe it, Tucker?—S & M retreat centers abroad supplied with drugs and erotic stimulants! That's the 'overseas ventures' Rigore must have heard them talking about! God forbid, Tucker, that Mrs. Castleton ever learns about this. Imagine, S & M retreat centers equipped with erotic stimulants, and funded with Castleton money!"

Tucker managed to keep his composure as Isadora continued, "Rigore keeps in touch with the Tittely sisters, whom you recall, Tucker. They offered that course about affectional transferences with a back-and-forth title no one can ever remember. Well, the poor twins haven't been able to find steady employment since. And they were being paid out of a special bequest from Mrs. Castleton. Longshot, you see, stole the money intended for them!"

"So," Isadora concluded, "this is why I needed to inform you, Tucker. Rigore Mortisse is kindly advising the twins to file a lawsuit against Longshot, and he thinks they would have a stronger case if they could get others of us, including me and certainly you, to make this a joint action. But my concern is over what it would mean to make all this public. They have agreed to do nothing further until I could speak with you. I thought you would have access to advice from the lawyers of the Castleton Trust as how best to proceed."

Tucker thanked Isadora for informing him of these reports and particularly for agreeing that the whole matter remain confidential, as he stressed, until he could consult with the Castleton attorneys and report back to her at the earliest convenience. Isadora thanked him in turn, adding, "It's amazing, isn't it, what academic research can turn up?"

Episode 36

A Graduation Announcement

WITH TUCKER'S QUICK ACTIONS Broadside's suspicions had been allayed by his having arranged a gratifying individual meeting for her with the Castleton attorneys who assured her in solemn confidentiality that President Longshot was actually taking a leave of absence to make up for any financial losses by establishing new spiritual and meditation retreat centers abroad for pilgrimages to renowned sacred areas. Because natural health products would be available to those seeking healing benefits at some of these retreat centers the badly misinformed false rumors had undoubtedly arisen. The professor was highly commended for coming forward right away in her determination to put a stop to such outrageously slanderous charges and for not allowing them to advance further.

To this adulation Isadora had responded that she was immensely relieved but not at all surprised to learn the truth as she hadn't herself believed for one moment any of the rumors she was reporting but definitely felt it her duty to prevent their circulating, knowing, she added, how destructive such gossip can be. As they were about to adjourn in this contrived conviviality one of the attorneys was handed a personal message just phoned in from Mrs. Castleton at Tucker's instigation and hastily transcribed by an office staff assistant containing her request that it be read aloud before Professor Broadside departed. Expressing appreciation for Broadside's devoted service to the seminary, the lady asked as a personal favor that the professor honor the coming end of term graduation ceremonies at Star-Cross with one of her appalling (misspelled for "appealing") lute selections. After an instant of nervous laughter all around and the embarrassed reader profusely offering apologies for not catching the misspelling in the transcribed note before speaking it, Isadora undeterred departed in high spirits, reporting later to Tucker excitedly how she had received a personal invitation from no less than Mrs. Castleton herself to perform a lute solo at graduation and how her highly confidential special meeting with the Trust legal advisors had proved most successful in providing information to counteract false accusations of defamation being spread against President Longshot with the possible harm they could cause to the seminary. Inspirited by her Castleton endorsements it was apparent that the now devalued hearsay of Mortisse had become for Isadora small change indeed.

A further enticement to guarantee Broadside's continued compliance should it prove necessary Tucker had also discussed with the concerned benefactor. Castleton funds would be made available to finance the publishing of a correctly titled reissue of Isadora's *Luten Meditations for Peace Seeking Buddhists, with Floppy Disk*. But that announcement, they both agreed, would now best be held in reserve until later, "Allowing me sufficient time," the dear lady had whispered, "to remove my hearing aids."

In the remaining weeks leading up to graduation Mildred Castleton had stressed to Tucker her desire that Longshot's leaving, though under a cloud, be treated with the deference she thought that his years of tenure as President of Star-Cross deserved. After all, he had led the seminary from its infancy, and not denying the seriousness of his administrative failings, the seminary had also undoubtedly been shaped for good in some important respects by his influence. She was personally indebted to Longshot for making her more sensitive to the plight of Native Americans and primarily credited him for the eventual decision of the Castleton Trust to divest itself of all its ill-founded properties involving fracking on native sacred lands. For this and similar instances of raising awareness she had sought to make her tribute to her father's memory in the reconsecration of the Major's Chapel something that viewers would spontaneously recognize as also paying homage to President Longshot's governing philosophy as well, as Tucker no doubt realized, *The Spirit of Love from A to Z*. The President had, she conceded, been far too modest to acknowledge that this tribute to Major Castleton had also been designed to honor himself at the time the banner had been presented, but she was certain nevertheless that he was as aware of the honor being paid him by her selection as much as those were aware in attendance. "No doubt," Tucker had replied.

Seeking Angelica's advice, for only her and Batson could he call upon given the situation, a way of acknowledging Longshot's contribution had been devised that was acceptably deferential and yet at the same time not overstated and disingenuous. Why not, Angelica had suggested, invite all in the graduating class who wished to do so to compose and submit a *Haiku* epitomizing what they considered to be a major theme of Longshot's *pan-pneumatic* vision? Having heard the President often speak in his usual manner about both the spirituality of matter and the materiality of spirit with an emphasis upon metaphors of liquidity rather than solidity that allow, as one of his most characteristic phrases put it, a "destabilization of meaning" devoid of regulated exclusivity, how might this most aptly be distilled in a *Haiku's* only seventeen syllables of three consecutive lines consisting first of five syllables, then seven syllables, and then five concluding syllables that often make reference to some aspect of nature?

"You've got me," Batson had responded in their planning session, earning a look from the raised eyebrow of his not much longer to be student that she was not amused. Tucker had been impressed with the idea, found it brilliant, and shortly had the voluntary invitation sent to all in the graduating class. To stimulate incentive for participation Mildred Castleton had donated two five hundred dollar prizes for entries judged to be the best. All of them would be collected in a volume, signed by their authors, and presented to the President as a goodwill gesture upon undertaking his leave of absence.

In retrospect the graduation ceremonies would be remembered as having proceeded without incident thanks to ideal weather playing its part and no sudden disruptions marring the occasion. Longshot presiding as customary had introduced Daphne Doolittle who as Chair of the Board congratulated each graduate in the awarding of degrees and then announced Longshot's leave of absence and Tucker's appointment for the time being as Acting President. No one seemed much surprised at hearing the news of either. Tucker was generally viewed by both faculty and students alike as a most favorable stand-in. Following a brief presentation to Longshot of the graduating class's book of composed *Haiku* verses, a respectable number having been submitted, the two winners were announced and their prizes awarded. To the cheering approval and enjoyment of the audience, particularly the several Japanese in attendance, with everyone keeping count of the syllables, they read their verses.

> *Matter and Spirit*
> *Without formal boundaries.*
> *Rain dropping in air.*

> ––––––

> *Nothing exclusive*
> *In destabilization.*
> *Weeds seen as flowers.*

Broadside's rendition on her lute had gone longer than scheduled but was awarded a scattering of polite, if restless applause, as the eagerly anticipated time for ice cream and commencement picture taking propelled a move of the graduates and their guests toward the campus gardens where many would linger until the final promises of remaining in touch had been exchanged and the growing twilight had hastened the inevitable scattering of departures.

In bidding farewell and extending his genuine best wishes later in the week to his longtime associate before his imminent departure Tucker had ventured to share with Longshot what Mildred Castleton had told him about her intent to show her appreciation for the President by the choice she had made of the chapel reconsecration tribute to her father. Longshot had responded by saying only, "She is a good woman, but she was used. That's all past now. I am counting on you to be attentive to her while I am gone." His leave taking had proven to be a non-event with the only public notice being an unattributed one liner from the inside pages of a local paper betraying a tell tale sign of the reputed collusion between Rigore Mortisse and Longshot's office secretary by stating that the President of Star-Cross Seminary was "expiring" (*sic.*) temporarily in an effort to promote S and M retreat centers for tourists traveling abroad.

A new chapter for Star-Cross was clearly at hand, whether Tucker had initially felt prepared for it or not, and now having the needed time for reflection he found in the coming weeks his reinspired energies eagerly turning to it. Batson's book was completed and in the hands of the publisher, and Angelica after a brief vacation had taken up residence in an ideally situated apartment provided for her at the Castleton homeplace. She and Batson had begun immediately to examine together the information they had assembled regarding refugee assistance programs and had quickly been able to focus upon what looked to be the most desirable possibilities.

Mrs. Castleton was at her prime in the almost daily conferences she enjoyed with Angelica and had taken great interest in preparing for the next steps as their planning developed. These included not only the considerable paper work required by various agencies but the necessary appointment interviews conducted at her home of individuals with the recommended professional expertise needed to assist in the complex range of areas essential to their efforts. Within a relatively short time these interviews had expanded into a series of summer afternoon picnics which Mildred hosted on her lawn, bringing together a diverse and growing group of specialists and local volunteers committed to the project. Next steps also included, most importantly, the offer by Emmaus Church in town, where Batson in company with several others from Star-Cross often attended, even remarkably on occasion along with a self-professed None in disguise, of sufficient space within a wing of its own Social Hall with a separate entrance from the parking lot to be used as a public information and collection center for the receipt and storage of donations to the refugee relief undertaking. As news had spread in the community not all reactions to be sure had been favorable, but despite certain predictable local opposition against what was admittedly still a controversial undertaking, much good will had been expressed with the donations to date far exceeding expectations.

A keenly anticipated church supper that was open and welcoming to the public was now scheduled for the coming week to celebrate the success of this center and receive an update on how the refugee program was advancing. Angelica had gotten Tucker to agree to represent Star-Cross as Acting President in expressing appreciation to the Pastor and people for all their support and contributions. Driving back one afternoon from having spent much of another day in town working with others to ready the center, Angelica circled by the Star-Cross campus now mostly vacant in the summer where she had arranged to meet briefly with Batson to report on her day. Relaxing together in the Sacred Garden in the serenity of the Buddha's gaze they remarked of how haphazard life at Star-Cross could suddenly seem at times. "And still," Angelica added, "I often had a sense through all the craziness of trying to find our way that we were somehow being accompanied, we just never quite knew how to name it."

"Sounds like you've been reading the ancient mystics," Batson said. "Yes," Angelica replied, "and also your dissertation." Daring to lean close, Batson instantly clicked a selfie, and this time he did not ask, and Angelica did not object. She was no longer his student, and the Buddha was looking straight ahead.

Episode 37

On The Road to Emmaus

The sound of his phone ringing late in the night, or rather in the early hours of morning, startled Batson awake with the portent of bad news such untimely calls always bring. It was the Pastor of Emmaus calling to let him know that there had been a fire and to ask him to get the word to the others as soon as he thought best. "How bad?," Batson had asked, dreading to hear. "It could surely have been worse," the Reverend said. "Everyone fortunately was gone from the church, but the refugee collection center with everything stored in it has been totally destroyed, and much of the Social Hall which we had set up in preparation for our supper is in ashes as well." "Do they know what caused it?," Batson stammered, his body shaking, "How it could have happened?"

"Oh yes," the Reverend calmly said. "It was deliberate, an act of arson. Someone torched the place and left their hate slogans painted outside on the parking lot at the entrance. The police have the whole area cordoned off, but in their flood lights you can see that much from a distance."

Relaying the message to Tucker at once, Batson and he agreed that Angelica and Mrs. Castleton should not be disturbed until later after the sun was up, and that the two of them should go together to break the sad news to them personally. As it turned out, they both received calls shortly from Angelica telling them that a member of the housekeeping staff had heard reports on the local news and had awakened her to prepare to help assist Mrs. Castleton when she awoke. The three of them agreed to meet together at mid-morning when Angelica phoned them that the dear lady was ready to see them.

The call from Angelica came sooner than expected. Mrs. Castleton was up, had listened to the news, and now having finished a light breakfast, was looking to receive them. "She is determined that Clarence drive us all up there to be with the church people," Angelica whispered. "I don't know what we should do."

When Tucker and Batson arrived they were surprised to find Mildred seated at the entrance, erect and waiting for them with her hat and glasses, and her pocketbook in hand. Upon learning that they had not eaten breakfast she insisted they at least have a cup of coffee and a muffin. "Our main concern today must be for those church members and the local volunteers," she said. "Tucker, I'm sure I can trust you to know best how we can be supportive of them at this time."

Her repeated expressions of confidence in him proved too much at the moment, and speaking earnestly to her Tucker confessed that he must let her know he also had at times in the past played a part in taking advantage of her. Looking directly at him she replied in a gentle tone of mocked sternness, "Dr. T. Upton, when we know who we belong to, and why, nothing can take advantage of us. You do remember that first question of the old catechism, don't you?"

"*What is your only comfort in life and death?*," Tucker and Batson answered softly, reciting in unison as Mildred's eyes glistened in hearing quoted the once familiar words of the historic Reformed Heidelberg Catechism she had learned as a child.

Then summoning Clarence, in the cap Tucker had given him, to bring up the car she directed Tucker into the front seat with him, and with Mildred, Angelica, and Batson at his back, and the hope of Star-Cross riding with them, they turned onto the road together in the Chrysler, not knowing what awaited them, or what they would encounter on the way going to Emmaus.

Acknowledgments

MY THANKS ARE EXPRESSED to all the friends who responded to selected episodes, especially to Craig Berggren for insightful comments all along the way, to Jacqueline Outka for previewing portions of the completed text, to Nancy Duff for assistance in proof-checking typesets of the final copy, and to all the collaborative Wipf and Stock staff that had a hand in its publication.

80568682R00093

Made in the USA
Columbia, SC
08 November 2017